CU00909153

THE PORTAL ON CRANKLE LANE

IN THE SHADOW OF THE SPHINX

Watch the trailer: youtube.com/watch?v=Eu1BUZCSyvQ

Your free desktop wallpaper is waiting!

Get it at akwallis.com/free

To connect with the author:

www.akwallis.com
Facebook.com/akwallisauthor
Twitter.com/@akwallis113
Pinterest.com/akwallis0113
(here, you will find the book board for *In the Shadow of the Sphinx*)

THE PORTAL ON CRANKHALL LANE

IN THE SHADOW OF THE SPHINX

A. K. WALLIS

© AK WALLIS, 2017

All rights reserved. This book or any portion thereof may not be reproduced or used in any manner whatsoever without the express written permission of the author except for the use of brief quotations in a book review.

This is a work of fiction. Although parts of the book are based on factual places and historical figures, any names, characters, businesses, places, events and incidents are either the products of the author's imagination or used in a fictitious manner.

Cover design by Extended Imagery.
All hieroglyphs used inside the book are courtesy of JSesh Hieroglyphic Editor.

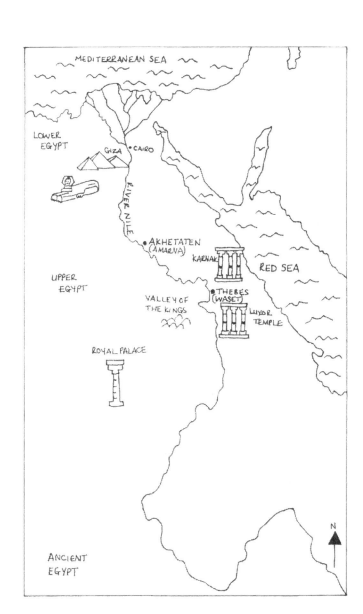

MEDITERRANEAN SEA

LOWER
EGYPT

GIZA
• CAIRO

RIVER NILE

• AKHETATEN
(AMARNA)

KARNAK

RED SEA

UPPER
EGYPT

VALLEY OF
THE KINGS

• THEBES
(WASET)

LUXOR
TEMPLE

ROYAL PALACE

N

ANCIENT
EGYPT

CHAPTER ONE

Eleven year old Charlie Swain turned into the street where he had lived all his life and stopped dead in his tracks. Ahead of him, at the very top of Crankhall Lane, was a small, cobbled alleyway he had never seen before. He was sure it hadn't been there when he walked to school that morning.

Charlie stood at the top of the alleyway and stared at it with a mixture of interest and confusion. Surely this alley hadn't been there all along. 'But then, how can an alley appear out of nowhere?' he asked himself. Charlie scratched his head and frowned. Had he really walked past this every day and not noticed it? Charlie thought it was unlikely, but it seemed the only explanation. After all, it really was very small and narrow. 'And my teachers are always telling me I don't pay enough attention,' thought Charlie. 'Perhaps they're right.'

The alley was short, so short in fact that Charlie was unsure whether it could be called an alley at all. Before him the narrow, cobbled passageway ended abruptly with a dead end. As is usual for alleyways, it was framed by walls on either side but, less usually, in the right hand wall Charlie could see a single, bay window. Even without going into the alley, it was clear that the window, made up of square panels of glass, was filled with books. He felt a rush of excitement at the realisation and wondered whether it was safe to follow his curiosity and step into the alley that had appeared as if from nowhere.

'It really is more likely,' Charlie decided, 'that I have never noticed it, than it is that someone put an alley and a shop here in no more time than a school day.' In any case, it was just a bookshop. And no harm ever came from going into a bookshop.

'Oi, Charlie!' A boy shouted down the street towards Charlie, who instantly recognised the voice and did his best to ignore it. 'Another rubbish performance in football today!'

Charlie kept his back to the voice and made his decision. Slowly, he took a cautious step into the alleyway, where he was greeted by the sight of a bright, red door in the wall next to the window.

'That's odd,' thought Charlie. 'I didn't notice the door when I saw the window.'

Charlie turned to face the door. To his left, a string of warm white fairy lights twinkled in the window filled with the books. In front of him, the red door was cheery and reminded him of Christmas. It didn't have a traditional handle but instead displayed a large, gold, oval-shaped ring with a cross shape attached to it.

'Oi, Charlie!' The voice from the street continued. 'Are you ignoring me?'

Charlie studied the ring on the door.

'Look at him!' said the voice. 'Just standing there, staring at the wall!'

'Forget it, Ben,' said another voice. 'Even his dad doesn't think he's worth the bother. He left him years ago!' And the voices turned to laughter as Charlie reached out and grabbed the ring on the door. It made a slight creaking noise as he twisted it slowly to the right, and then the door swung suddenly and violently open, pulling him through.

With surprise, Charlie stumbled into the shop and was greeted by a tall man with a bald head and an earring that resembled the ring on the door.

'Friends of yours?' asked the man, as the comments from the boys echoed down the alleyway.

'Not really,' Charlie answered quietly. 'Just boys from school.'

'They sound delightful.' The man gave a half smile to support his sarcasm and Charlie found himself smiling back.

The man's dark eyes were edged in what looked like black eyeliner. His jeans were slightly ripped at the knees, and he wore a t-shirt the same blue as the blazer of Charlie's school uniform. The clothes and the makeup and the earring seemed a strange combination.

'Is that an ankh?' Charlie pointed towards the man's earring, dangling from his earlobe. The oval loop attached to his ear ended with a cross.

'Indeed it is,' replied the man, bowing his head slightly as he did so. 'I assume you also recognised the same symbol on the door?'

Charlie nodded.

'So what can you tell me about the ankh?'

 The ankh

'It's an ancient Egyptian symbol,' said Charlie, enjoying the chance to show off some of his knowledge. 'It's the symbol that means 'life'. You find it in a lot of ancient

Egyptian tombs. No one really knows what the symbol actually is but some people think it's the shape of a sandal strap.'

'Excellent!' said the man, clearly impressed. 'So how do you know so much about ancient Egypt?'

'I love history,' said Charlie, his face lighting up. 'The more ancient, the better.'

The man chuckled. 'Excellent.'

They both fell quiet and Charlie felt the man staring at him with interest.

'So, your father has left?' asked the man, gesturing towards the open door as a reminder of where he had heard this piece of information.

Charlie suddenly felt awkward. 'Yeah,' he said, looking at the floor. 'He left me and my mom a few years ago - left us for another woman. He lives with her now, not far away actually. He has another son too. Apparently, he looks a bit like me.'

'Apparently?' asked the man, his one eyebrow raised in a pointed arch.

Charlie looked at the man and then back at the floor and nodded his head. 'I haven't met him myself. I haven't seen my dad for years.' He tried to make light of it and laughed a little as he spoke, 'My dad must prefer his other son!' He shrugged. 'It's no big deal.'

The man said nothing but he didn't take his eyes from Charlie, who felt the weight of his stare.

'Erm,' said Charlie, determined to break the silence, 'I've never seen your shop before, and I've lived here a long time.'

'We're what's called a pop up shop,' replied the man. 'We have appeared quickly and will only be here for a short time. It's all the rage,' he continued. 'Pop up shops are *popping up* everywhere!' He laughed at his own joke.

Charlie frowned. 'But what about the alley?' he asked the man. 'That can't have just *appeared*.'

The shopkeeper laughed again. 'It's amazing what we miss that's right under our noses!'

'I can't believe this alley was here the whole time and I didn't notice it,' Charlie thought to himself, and then he asked the man, 'Is it ok if I look around?'

'Be my guest.' The man stretched out a long finger, 'The ancient history section is over there.'

Charlie smiled. 'Thanks.'

'My pleasure.'

As Charlie headed towards the history section he could feel the man's eyes boring into his back, and the feeling only disappeared when he turned behind a set of shelves and found himself alone. From his place of safety, Charlie dropped his backpack on the floor and took the time to look around. To his right was the window he had seen from the alleyway but it was so full of books he could barely see through it to the alley beyond. The fairy lights continued with their twinkling and brought some additional light to the dark shop. The carpet too, was dark, it's brown pile doing nothing to brighten up the place. Everywhere there were shelves filled with books. The shelves stretched from floor to ceiling, and ladders were attached to them to help readers reach the books that sat up high. Behind Charlie was a large, dark wooden table, itself covered with piles of books. Nothing in the place seemed new, including the books themselves which, from the look of them, were all old and used. The shop had the musty smell of somewhere that had spent too long locked up from all daylight and fresh air. In the odd shaft of light that made its way through the window and into the shop, dust floated gently.

In spite of, or perhaps because of, its strangeness, Charlie liked the shop. He made a mental note to tell his mom about it so she would have time to visit before the owner moved on. And then, high above his head, at the top of the shelves that towered immediately above him, Charlie's eyes saw a sign that brought a familiar fizzle of excitement up from his very feet. It read simply, 'AN-CIENT WORLD.'

Charlie took a deep breath and allowed his eyes to scan the rows of books before him, all of them filled with knowledge about ancient Egypt, and Greece, and Rome, about the Assyrians and the Babylonians, about some of the most famous people ever to have walked the Earth, and about stories that had lasted through millennia. He didn't know where to start.

Charlie slowly ran his finger along the spines of the books level with his eye line and stopped on a book with nothing on its spine except a small row of hieroglyphs. Intrigued, Charlie began to pull the book out from the shelf but a sudden noise made him stop, and he jumped instead. The noise was a loud thud, and it was followed by a plume of dust that arose upwards from a spot on the carpet next to Charlie's feet, surrounding him and making him cough. He waved his hand around in the air and when the dust finally cleared, Charlie looked in the direction of the thud. There, at his feet, lay a large, leather bound book. Charlie looked from the book, to the shelf, and back to the book again. Not for the first time this afternoon, Charlie scratched his head in confusion. He had no idea where the book had come from. He looked back to the book he had begun to pull from the shelf and saw that it was still sitting there, packed tightly in amongst the others that shared its resting place; there was no space from where the book at his feet could have fallen. Frowning, he scanned the rest of the shelves around him, looking for a gap that had once belonged to the book that had thudded onto the floor, but there was none.

'Is everything ok?' The man shouted from the front of the shop.

'Erm, it's fine, thank you!' Charlie shouted back.

Charlie stared again at the book, still lying on the floor. And as he stared the worn cover appeared to change before his eyes. Charlie scrunched his eyes shut tight and then rubbed them but when he looked back, the book's changing cover was still there. As his eyes focused on the book, it seemed to Charlie that the midnight blue leather began to shimmer, whilst vague, gold images he couldn't quite make out moved in and out of view on the book's cover in perfect rhythm. Charlie looked at the window. 'Is it the light playing tricks?' he wondered. The more he stared at the book, the more it seemed to come to life and now Charlie could see ancient Egyptian hieroglyphs all over the front cover.

Charlie took a step back, feeling afraid. What kind of book was this? Cautiously, he leant in again to take another look, but this time the book seemed like any other in the shop, old and dusty, with no sign of a moving cover. Charlie smiled to himself in relief. It must have been the light after all!

He bent down and picked up the book from the floor. Its cover was worn and bits of midnight blue leather had peeled away at the edges, revealing gold patches beneath. Charlie set the book down on the table behind him, doing his best to do it as quietly as possible so as not to draw attention from the shopkeeper. After a quick glance over his shoulder to be sure he was alone, he pulled a chair up to the table and slowly opened the book.

Charlie's mind was spinning with ideas of all that could lie within its pages. He couldn't wait to find out what was inside, and he realised he was holding his breath as he pulled back the cover. Eagerly, he looked down at the first page, barely able to contain his excitement. Yet, instead of a fascinating world, Charlie discovered only disappointment. Instead of exciting things about the ancients, Charlie was faced with only blank pages. He turned over more of them, eventually opening the book in the middle, and then turning right to the back in the hope of finding a page that wasn't empty, but all he found were blank stares.

'How can a book be empty?' Charlie whispered to himself as he leant back in his chair, deflated.

'Find anything interesting?'

For the second time this afternoon Charlie jumped in surprise, this time as the man's voice cut through his concentration.

'I'm sorry,' laughed the man as Charlie instinctively placed his hand to his heart.

'You scared me!'

'Did you find something interesting?' asked the man again, repeating his question and staring down at the book in front of Charlie on the table.

'I thought I had,' answered Charlie. 'But it's blank!'

'Are you sure? I don't think anyone would bother to make a blank book.'

'I'm sure! Look!' Charlie leafed through some of the pages to prove to the man he was telling the truth.

'Many things seem different from their true nature,' said the man. 'Everywhere we are surrounded by things we cannot see or hear, but that does not mean they are not there. What does the wind look like? Or a thought? We cannot see either one but we know they exist. What does a dog whistle sound like? The only way for us to know of their existence is to look for their effects. Yet the leaves know the wind exists because they feel it rustling through them. The dog knows the whistle makes a real noise because it can hear it and responds. Things are not always as they seem. Just because you do not see them does not mean they are not there. You, for instance, have never seen this alleyway before, and yet here we are.'

The man put his hand up to his ear and began playing with the ankh earring. 'In any case,' he said, 'if the book really is blank, then it is of no use to me. Why don't you take it Charlie? You never know what you might learn from it.'

Charlie's eyes widened and he began to feel afraid. The shop was silent. Charlie couldn't even hear noise from the street. They could have been anywhere. 'How do you know my name?' he asked the man, trying to stand from his chair but his legs refusing to obey.

'Your name?' The man's eyes looked straight back into Charlie's, not so much as blinking.

'Yes,' Charlie swallowed. 'How do you know my name?'

The man laughed and then waved his hand around theatrically. 'I heard those boys shouting it when you came into the shop, of course!' He stared back at Charlie, a half smile on his face. 'How else would I know it?'

'I think I should go,' said Charlie, managing to stand and beginning to make his way to the front of the shop.

'Don't you want your book?'

'Erm, no, thank you.'

'Oh come on,' said the man light heartedly. 'I'm giving it to you for free. It's no use here. It may as well go to a good home. Maybe you can use it for a journal or something.'

The man held out the book but Charlie just stared at it, unsure what to do for the best.

'Take the book Charlie,' said the man again, but this time there was an authority in his voice that made Charlie do as he was asked.

'Thank you,' said Charlie as he took the book and rushed towards the shop door.

'You're very welcome,' said the shopkeeper. 'I hope to see you again soon.'

Charlie managed a half smile and made his way back out into the alleyway. He headed straight for the street, stopping only when he was back on the familiar pavement of Crankhall Lane and in full view of traffic, houses and passers by. He leant against a wall, clutching the book to his chest and allowing his breathing to return to normal. The strange encounter with the shopkeeper had made his heart beat faster.

Eventually, Charlie began to feel calm again and as he leant up from the wall, ready to head home, he realised in a panic that he had left his school bag in the shop.

'Oh, no,' said Charlie, groaning to himself. 'Now I have to go back in.'

Charlie sighed as he wondered whether going back inside the shop was a good idea, and he turned around to look in the direction of the alleyway. As he did, the shock of what he saw caused him to drop the book from his arms and his mouth to fall open. In front of him was no alley-way, and no shop, but only a brick wall where the alley had been. And against the wall was a single item. As he stared in disbelief, Charlie saw not the alleyway he expected to see but instead a backpack. Against the brick wall, where the alleyway had been, was nothing but Charlie's blue schoolbag.

CHAPTER TWO

Charlie tumbled through the front door to his house and ran straight upstairs to his bedroom.

'Is that you Charlie?'

'Yes, Mom!'

'Well it's a good job you're heading up those stairs, Charlie Swain! I've seen the state of your room, and tonight you're going to clean it!'

Charlie didn't respond. Instead he slammed the door shut behind him and sat down on his bed. In front of him on the floor was his school bag, and in it was the book. Charlie chewed on his thumbnail and thought nervously about everything that had happened that afternoon. He thought about the alleyway and the shop, he thought about the book and the shopkeeper, and he thought about how the alley had somehow been there one minute and gone the next.

'It's unbelievable,' Charlie said aloud to his empty room. 'Maybe I'm losing my mind.' And suddenly Charlie felt afraid. 'What if there's something wrong with me?' The thought made him run downstairs to the one place he always felt safe.

'Mom,' he said, heading straight for the kitchen and looking at her with big eyes.

His mom was stood on tiptoes trying to reach for a tin of tomatoes from a cupboard in the kitchen that had always been just a little too high for her. She looked around as he came into the kitchen. 'Don't think for even one minute that you're going to get out of cleaning that r...' Her voice trailed off and her face took on a look of concern as she saw Charlie's own, worried look. 'What's wrong?'

Charlie threw himself towards her and hugged her tightly. 'Nothing, I'm fine,' he lied. He wouldn't even know where to begin to explain what had happened today. 'I love you, Mom.' Charlie felt a lump in his throat. I'd hate it if I ever lost you.'

'Hey, come on now,' she replied, releasing the hug so she could look him in the eye. 'What's brought this on?'

Charlie looked into the brown eyes that mirrored his own. 'Nothing really,' he said, shaking his head. 'It's just, Dad...' He didn't finish the sentence, unsure how.

'Listen to me, Charlie.' His mom placed a hand on each of his shoulders to show she meant what she was about to say. 'I am not going anywhere. Ever.'

Charlie believed her, but he feared it might happen all the same.

'Ok?' his mom asked him.

He looked into the face of the person he trusted most in the world and saw she meant every word. 'Ok,' he said, nodding.

'Good,' his mom replied. 'Unless, of course, you don't do something about that room of yours. Then I might have to move out, your things are practically spilling out into the rest of the house!'

Charlie laughed. His mom always made him feel better. Somehow she always made it seem as though his fears were nothing much to worry about after all.

'Well, I'm glad you're laughing about it. Now go and do something about it! You've got half an hour until dinner. I'll come up and tell you when it's ready.'

What she meant by that, Charlie knew, was that she would be coming upstairs in half an hour to check he had cleaned his room as she had asked. Dropping his shoulders as he resigned himself to the task before him, he turned around and headed back upstairs.

When he reached his room, he stood staring at the mess before him and realised it was going to take a lot longer than half an hour to sort it out. Groaning at the thought, he sighed and flopped dramatically down onto his unmade bed, before rolling onto his back and looking up at the ceiling - at least that was a clean, tidy space. As long as he continued to look upwards, he could begin to convince himself that the rest of the room was just as clear of clutter. As he lay there, the mattress and covers beneath him began to form to his shape and made him feel sleepy. And he needed a rest after the day he'd had. Aside from the strange incident at the bookshop, today was also Wednesday, and Charlie hated school on a Wednesday. It was a day filled with all of his least favourite lessons: double maths and double physics in the morning, and biology, followed by P.E. of all things, in the afternoon. Charlie was just glad he had managed to get through another Wednesday and wouldn't have to face it again for a whole week.

'Charlie Swain, I hope you're tidying your room and not just lying on that bed of yours!'

His mom's voice carried up the stairs and made him sit up. Could she see through walls? 'I am, Mom!'

'Ok then. Half an hour.'

Charlie made a half-hearted attempt to extract a dirty plate from the floor beside his bed and found that he was able to lift it by simply picking up the fork that had become welded to its surface. He amused himself for a moment, laughing as he waved the plate around in the air whilst holding only the fork's handle, and then he sighed and dropped the plate back onto the floor as he realised again just how much tidying he was going to have to do.

He looked around him. His chest of drawers had three of its four drawers open, with jumpers and t-shirts and socks hanging out of them. His bookcase held an array of books all sat at different angles to one another, some barely hanging onto the shelf. The dark blue carpet on his floor was littered with more books, as well as magazines, colouring pencils, and clothes that he hadn't been bothered to put in the washing basket. Beneath his bed were dusty, untidy piles of board games he hadn't played for at least the last four years, and old colouring books and spot the difference books that were spilling out onto his red, white and blue striped rug. At the edges of his bed, half underneath and half out in the room, were a couple of unwashed cups, that had once contained orange squash, to accompany the plate he had already found. Beside his bed, his desk stood completely covered with all kinds of papers, books, toys and other random items, all piled precariously on top of each other, making it at once foolish to make any sudden movements and impossible to use his desk - he had been doing his homework whilst sat on his bed for several weeks now.

The only things in Charlie's room that were just as they should be were the walls. The walls were, in Charlie's opinion, perfectly decorated. From his bed, he looked, as he often did, at the images that hung there and, as always, his eyes sparkled with excitement. Staring back at him were images of gladiators and Greek warriors, of Egyptian tombs and Greek temples, of Roman amphitheatres and ancient sites and cities from all across the world. Anyone who stepped for just a short time into Charlie's room and who knew his school timetable would instantly have been able to tell that whilst Charlie Swain's least favourite day at school was Wednesday, his favourite part of the school week was a Friday afternoon. It's true that this is the favourite part of the week for many school goers who are eagerly awaiting the start of the weekend, but for Charlie there was another reason to celebrate that particular time in his week: Friday afternoon was double history.

Charlie's history teacher, Mr Cook, had once commented that he had never known anyone so enthusiastic about the subject. He had also pointed out in a particular lesson when Charlie was enthralling two of his classmates with tales of ancient Rome, that whilst Charlie's imagination was one of his greatest gifts, there was little place for imagination in the pursuit of history's truths. History required logical thinking and sensible conclusions formed from the evidence, not the creation of stories, however entertaining they may be.

'Charlie, dinner's almost ready! You've got ten minutes. I'll come up and tell you when it's done.'

'Ok, Mom!' Charlie shouted back before dropping his shoulders in defeat. 'I'll never get this done in ten minutes,' he thought to himself.

As he prepared himself for the telling off he was almost certainly going to receive, his eyes locked onto another set looking back at him from his window sill. The dark eyes that stared at him were edged in blue and looked out from a face covered in gleaming gold and surrounded by deep blue stripes. The owner of the eyes wore a strange looking headdress, on which a vulture sat at the side of a cobra, both looking out in the same direction. Somewhere below the headdress and the eyes, and beneath a gold nose and mouth, was a long beard. The small replica of Tutankhamun's death mask had been in Charlie's room for so long now that the pair of eyes looking back at him felt like those of a friend. The item was one of Charlie's most prized possessions, brought to England for him by his auntie Mariam on one of her visits home. Like his auntie, the ornament had come all the way from Cairo itself.

'Tell me about Egypt, Auntie Mariam,' Charlie had asked excitedly when she arrived home. 'Tell me all about the pyramids and the desert, and about the tombs in the Valley of the Kings. Tell me about the pharaohs and the gods and the temples and monuments covered in hieroglyphs!'

'At least let me take off my coat first!' she had said good naturedly, laughing as she handed her coat to Charlie's mom, who took it and filled Auntie Mariam's now empty hands with a hot mug of tea.

Auntie Mariam had thanked her sister with a smile and then sat down at the kitchen table. Charlie had scampered after her, climbing into the chair opposite his auntie and begging to be told every little detail about Egypt.

'Before I answer your questions, I've got something for you,' Auntie Mariam had said as she reached into her sizeable handbag and pulled out a parcel. 'Here,' she had said, pushing the parcel across the table towards Charlie.

Charlie remembered pulling at the string and ripping excitedly into the parcel paper, before drawing a sharp intake of breath as he first looked into the same pair of eyes that were looking back at him now.

Charlie had his auntie Mariam to thank for his love of history. She emailed him regularly and called him every so often on Skype, updating him with what was going on where she worked at the Egyptian Museum in Cairo. Even after all this time, he still couldn't contain his excitement when he received a new email or a call or, even better, news that his auntie Mariam was coming home on a visit.

'Do you remember the day we first met, Tut?' he said to the statue. The eyes continued to look intently back at him.

Charlie sighed again as he realised there was nothing even remotely interesting or exciting about having to clean his room. His mom, he knew, would be coming upstairs in a matter of minutes under the guise of fetching him for dinner but, as both she and Charlie knew, it was really to check that he had cleaned his room as she had asked. Clearly, he hadn't.

'It's no good, Tut,' he said to the Pharaoh looking back at him with apparent interest. 'It'll never be done.' But then, in a flash of inspiration a thought popped into Charlie's head. 'Of course! It's ok Tut, I have an idea!' Then, as quickly as he was able, he got to work - there wasn't much time.

Ten minutes later, Charlie heard his mom begin to climb the stairs. When she came into his room, Charlie was sitting on his bed, with his back against the wall, reading a book and feeling pretty pleased with himself. His mom looked surprised.

'I said I would tidy it up, Mom.'

His mom didn't seem to know quite what to say. 'I know you did, it's just...'

Charlie looked at her in mock disappointment, apparently hurt that she hadn't really expected his room to be tidy. 'It's just what, Mom?'

The look on her face was replaced with one of guilt. 'Nothing,' she said, shaking her head. 'It looks lovely in here. It's very tidy, Charlie. Well done for doing such a good job.'

Charlie smiled, truly proud of himself.

'Grandad's out with a friend tonight, so it's just the two of us. Are you ready for dinner?'

Charlie nodded.

'I'll just hang this up before we go downstairs.' In one quick movement, Charlie's mom picked up the coat he had left on the bottom of his bed and placed her hand on the cupboard handle. Charlie leant forward in panic but before he could say or do anything to stop her, his mom had pulled open the cupboard door.

What happened next felt to Charlie as if it were happening in slow motion. There were several loud crashes as piles of items of all kinds flung themselves out of the cupboard that had been stuffed so full Charlie had barely been able to close the door. One by one, and sometimes several at a time, the items fell with a thud onto the floor. Book after book, unwashed jumper after unwashed jumper, sock after sock, board game after board game spilled out and surrounded Charlie's mom, who stood there speechless, watching as the pile around her grew. Just when Charlie thought the commotion had finished, a final object slid out of the cupboard and landed at his mom's feet. Both Charlie and his mom watched it fall and stared at it as it came to rest on the floor. Next to his mom's right foot was a plate, with a fork forever welded to its surface.

Charlie looked at the floor, covered once more in mess and clutter, and then offered his mom an uncertain smile.

His mom looked unimpressed. She said nothing but instead responded with a single, raised eyebrow.

CHAPTER THREE

It was after dinner and Charlie found himself back in his room with strict orders to clean up the mess. And once again, Charlie was doing anything he could to avoid the inevitable.

'You've got half an hour, Charlie. And then I'm coming up to make sure that room is spotless!'

'Yes, Mom!' Charlie rolled his eyes as he shouted back. 'Why do I have to clean it anyway?' he thought to himself. 'It'll only get messy again.'

Truth be told, Charlie wasn't all that bothered by the mess. He quite liked doing his homework whilst sat on his bed instead of at his desk, after all, it was comfier, and the various books, magazines and pencils that usually lay strewn across his bedroom floor were not, Charlie was sure, evidence of laziness so much as proof that when he got a new idea, he acted on it immediately. He simply didn't have the time to tidy away one thing before taking out another. If anything, Charlie thought, his messy room was the result of an inquisitive and creative mind. His mom disagreed.

Begrudgingly, Charlie bent down to pick up the plate with the attached fork that he had first retrieved from beneath his bed and that had later thrown itself at his mom's feet from out of his cupboard. As he stood again, the plate still hanging from the fork, he saw something that was infinitely more interesting: his school bag, with the book inside, stood next to his desk. Dropping the plate back onto the floor with a thud, Charlie threw himself onto his bed, made himself comfy and pulled his bag up towards him.

'I'll just take two minutes to have another look at it,' he said to himself. He unzipped his bag and placed his hand around the leather bound book just as his mom came into the room, and he quickly snatched his hand from his bag.

'Charlie,' was all his mom said, but the tone and the head shake were enough for him to know how much she disapproved of his choice to sit on his bed rather than clean up the mess in his room. She offered him a look that dared him to be sitting down rather than tidying up the next time she came into the room, and he immediately got to his feet. His mom left and Charlie looked from the bedroom door, through which his mom would certainly reappear shortly, to his backpack, now lying on his bed. He made a move back towards his bag just as he heard his mom's voice again.

'Charlie.'

It was nothing short of a warning and Charlie looked around him, certain that his mom must be able to see him somehow. Shaking his head at the silliness of his thought but too nervous to test the theory, Charlie decided the best course of action was to clean his room as quickly as possible so that he would finally be left in peace to examine his new book.

*****

At 8:30pm Charlie climbed into bed.

'Goodnight, Charlie. See you in the morning.'

'Night, Mom.'

His mom smiled and looked around his now tidy room. 'Doesn't it feel better when everything's put neatly away and you can get into bed without running an obstacle course first?'

Charlie was still unhappy that he had spent his evening cleaning and he was not about to let his mom think that she had been right, so he said nothing and yawned instead.

'Try and keep it this neat,' his mom said as she gently closed his bedroom door.

Charlie listened as she made her way back downstairs, and he kept listening until he heard her go into the living room and close the door behind her. He waited a couple of minutes, just to make sure everything was quiet and then, certain that he was alone upstairs, he sat up, reached hurriedly over for his school bag, which stood leaning against his desk, and excitedly opened it up. Unwilling to climb out from beneath the warmth of his covers and turn on the light, he struggled to see clearly but reasoned that his eyes would soon adjust to the dark room.

Using two hands, he pulled the book from his backpack and rested it on the bed covers that lay across his outstretched legs. It looked as it had in the shop, large and leather bound, its dark blue cover staring blankly back at him. He touched it with caution, but then reminded himself that the moving cover he had seen in the shop had been nothing but a trick of the light. He ran his hand over the blank cover wondering, just as he had in the shop, the point of an empty book. The leather was cool and smooth, and his fingers glided easily across its surface. Suddenly Charlie stopped in his tracks and frowned. Beneath his fingers he could feel something on the surface of the cover. 'What is *that*?' Charlie whispered to himself.

Feeling nervous, Charlie stretched over to grab the curtain. He forced his arm to extend as far as possible, just managing to grasp the corner of the fabric, which he pulled back, allowing the moon to bring light to the room.

From the window sill, Tutankhamun peered out, the silver moonlight causing the death mask to take on an eerie quality. Charlie looked from Tutankhamun to the book and felt his heart rate rise. His eyes grew wide as he looked down at the cover, and he had to remind himself to breathe. He leant in closer to be sure his eyes were telling him the truth and then, realising that they were, he leant back again and placed his hand across his mouth. Before his very eyes, the book cover that had been empty of all writing and images was no longer blank. Instead, across the centre of the front cover, in large letters that were both embossed into the leather and printed in gold, a title had appeared. It read simply:

THE PORTAL ON CRANKHALL LANE

Charlie stared at the title. Feeling afraid, he snatched the book up from his bed covers and bundled it back into his schoolbag, zipping the backpack tightly shut and pushing it beneath his bed where he could no longer see it. He lay back in his bed and pulled the covers up over his nose and mouth, his eyes peering out into the room. The curtains were still open but the silver light that streamed into the room only created shadows on the walls and made him feel all the more nervous. He tried to think about something else but all he could think about was the book, lying beneath his bed and zipped up in his schoolbag. He fixed his eyes on the ceiling and tried to remind himself that books are harmless items, but try as he might he couldn't shake the feeling that something strange was happening. And he knew that sleep would be impossible.

CHAPTER FOUR

Up in his room, Charlie heard the letterbox snap shut in the hallway as the day's post fell onto the mat. Any minute he knew he would hear, as he did every morning, his grandad walk into the hall from the kitchen and pick up the mail, before taking it with him back into the kitchen and looking through it as he ate his breakfast.

Feeling tired from the worst night's sleep he could remember, Charlie looked with suspicion through blurry eyes at his school bag. He chewed on his bottom lip as he wondered whether he dared to unzip his backpack and take another look at the book. 'Did I dream it?' he wondered.

Cautiously, Charlie reached forward and unzipped his bag. As he pulled it open, he could see the top of the book, its pages squashed together between its covers.

'Charlie!' His grandad shouted up to him from the hallway and made him jump. 'Charlie! Come and have your breakfast!'

Charlie never removed his eyes from the book as he shouted back. 'It's ok, Grandad! I'm not really hungry!'

'But you'll...' his grandad gave up. 'Well ok, if you want to get to school and then have to be hungry all morning!'

Charlie had stopped listening. Slowly, he placed his hand into his bag and then instantly withdrew it again. 'Ouch!' He looked at the source of the pain and saw a small droplet of blood appear on his middle finger. Inside his bag, a folded piece of paper had sliced into his skin.

He sucked at his finger to stop the bleeding and then, with extra caution, placed his hand back into his backpack and pulled out the book. In the cold light of day, Charlie half expected to see nothing but a blank cover but as he placed the book on his desk, he saw the same letters he had seen last night looking back at him. 'The Portal on Crankhall Lane,' he read aloud, running his fingers across the lettering. And then, holding his breath, he pulled open the book's cover. What he saw inside made him gasp. With his eyes firmly fixed on the book, he reached his hand out to feel for the back of his chair. When his hand found it, he pulled the chair out from beneath the desk before clumsily sitting down.

Charlie couldn't believe his eyes as he glared at the first page, which now held an image of a golden scarab beetle, framed by a deep border of ancient Egyptian hieroglyphs. Through the years he had learnt enough about ancient Egypt to know that the scarab was sacred. Also called a dung beetle, the scarab was associated with the Egyptian sun god, Amun-Ra. Just as the beetle pushed balls of dung across the desert floor, the sun god pushed the sun across the sky each day.

In each corner of the large page was an ankh symbol, the familiar oval loop with a cross beneath it that the man in the bookshop had worn dangling from his ear. Beneath the scarab with its hieroglyphic border, was an eye. The eye had a deep eyebrow above it and beneath it, a line extended downwards and ended with a swirl.

'The Eye of Horus,' Charlie whispered.

'Charlie! It's time for school!' Charlie felt irritation as he was reminded that he had a whole school day ahead. All Charlie wanted to do was stay at home and explore this book that had somehow started off blank and now had a title and images within it, all of which had appeared out of nowhere, just like the bookshop itself.

'Charlie!' his grandad shouted to him again. 'You'll be late!'

Charlie hurriedly closed the book and pushed it under his bed as far as he could. 'Coming!' He grabbed his blazer from the bottom of his bed and ran down the stairs ready for his grandad to drop him off at school. He really wished he didn't have to go - he had more important (and far more exciting) things to think about.

Charlie made his way out to his grandad's shiny, red car and climbed into the passenger seat. Even though the car was years old, it was kept so clean it smelt like new.

'Seatbelt, please,' his grandad instructed him, pulling on his own seatbelt and adjusting the rear view mirror.

Grandad liked everything to be just right, and Charlie loved that about him. It always made him feel so safe. He knew he could count on Grandad to get things right.

'Here,' said his grandad, throwing him a small, white, padded envelope and giving him a knowing look. 'This came for you this morning. It's got the Egyptian Museum stamp on it.'

'Auntie Mariam!'

Charlie ripped eagerly into the envelope and pulled out a card that had a short message on it. *Just a little something I picked up in Cairo recently. I saw it and thought of you. A. M. x*

He read the note and then tipped the envelope upside down, unable to contain his excitement.

'What have you got there?'

Charlie watched as a small item on a leather cord fell from the envelope. He picked up the cord and held up the item for his grandad to see. 'It's a scarab,' said Charlie, in awe. 'Auntie Mariam sent me a scarab!'

'So she did,' replied his grandad encouragingly, as Charlie placed the cord around his neck. The deep blue scarab beetle almost blended in with his blue school jumper.

'You'll need to put that inside your shirt,' advised his grandad. 'They won't let you wear that at school.'

Charlie admired the scarab, its underneath marked with a row of hieroglyphs. 'I wonder what they say?' he thought to himself. And then he pushed the pendant inside his shirt.

'Off we go!' said his grandad with a smile as he pulled out of their drive and headed off along Crankhall Lane towards the main road. When they reached the top of the street, Charlie looked out to see if he could spot the alleyway with the bookshop, but instead all he saw was a solid, brick wall. Feeling confused, Charlie leant back in his chair and continued to look out of the window, but he paid little attention to the houses and trees and other cars whizzing past. Instead, he was thinking about the book - and the bookshop. That is, until something, or rather someone, grabbed his attention. As they headed towards Charlie's school, Charlie saw a man walking along the street towards the nearby nursery school. A toddler gripped the man's hand and was laughing and skipping joyously along the street beside him.

Charlie looked at his grandad to see if he too had noticed, but if he had he said nothing about the fact that they had just driven past Charlie's dad with his new son. Charlie looked down at his fingers in his lap and picked at his nails.

'Do you miss Grandma?' he asked his grandad.

His grandad nodded. 'Every day.'

'Do you ever stop missing someone?' Charlie asked.

'That depends.'

'On what?'

'On whether they were good for you in the first place.'

Charlie fell quiet and then changed the subject. 'Do you miss Egypt, Grandad?'

His grandad smiled. 'Sometimes,' he said. 'I miss your auntie Mariam more. I like it best when my family are all together.'

Charlie nodded. 'I haven't had a call from Auntie Mariam for a while. That means she'll be in touch soon.'

'You can count on it,' his grandad replied. 'She loves telling you all about Egypt and the museum.'

Charlie nodded. 'So you are Egyptian, Grandad?'

'That's right, yes,' his grandad agreed.

'But Grandma was English?'

'That's right.'

'So what does that make Mom and Auntie Mariam and me?'

'Well,' said his grandad. 'Your mom and auntie are half Egyptian. You have one Egyptian grandparent, so that makes you one quarter Egyptian.'

Charlie loved being part Egyptian. 'I'd love to see Egypt, Grandad. I'd love to see the place you grew up.'

'I've always said I will take you there, Charlie. And I promise I will take you someday soon.'

Charlie grew excited at the thought. He turned to face his grandad, who kept his dark eyes on the road ahead. 'Do you like living with me and Mom?'

'I like nothing better,' he replied. After your grandma died, I was lonely and after...well, everything that happened...' His grandad looked awkward.

'You mean, after Dad left?' Charlie asked.

'Exactly,' said his grandad, sounding relieved that Charlie had said it and he didn't have to be the one to remind his grandson of a painful memory. 'After that, your mom asked if I wanted to live with the two of you. Which has worked out well, don't you think?'

Charlie nodded, enthusiastically. Living with his grandad was the best.

'I'm not lonely anymore, I get to spend lots of time with you and your mom, and I can drop you off at school when your mom is doing an early shift.'

They turned a corner and Charlie saw his school ahead. His grandad slowed down and pulled the car into a parking space opposite the school gate.

'Do you think Mom likes being a nurse?' Charlie asked his grandad.

'Yes, I do,' he replied.

'But Auntie Mariam prefers history, just like me?'

Charlie's grandad chuckled. 'That's right,' he said. 'She prefers history, just like you.'

'What do you prefer, Grandad?' Charlie asked as he opened the car door and started to climb out.

'Well, don't tell your mom,' he whispered, smiling at his grandson. 'But I prefer history too.'

Charlie smiled. 'See you tonight, Grandad.'

His grandad nodded. 'Have a good day.'

*****

That afternoon, Charlie was back at home after a frustrating day. He had found it impossible to concentrate and had been told off more than once for his inattentiveness. At break time, he had begun talking to his three best friends about the book, but the bell had gone to signal the start of the afternoon's lessons before he had had enough time.

Knowing that the book was at home waiting for him had made the day pass slower than ever, but now Charlie was back home and sitting at his desk, with the book in front of him once more. With an orange juice beside him, and knowing he wouldn't be disturbed because his mom and grandad thought he was doing his homework, Charlie opened the now familiar cover, ready to find out what else lay within.

He glanced for just a moment at the first page, with the scarab and the hieroglyphs and the ankh symbols and the Eye of Horus, and then he turned over to see if the book held any more images. What Charlie found next, he could never have predicted.

Charlie Swain of Crankhall Lane stumbled upon a bookstore at the top of his street. He had never seen it before but, as he is a boy with a healthy sense of curiosity, he decided to step inside. He opened the door, hearing the spiteful shouts of the boys from school as they teased him…

Charlie gasped. There, before his very eyes, the book which had just yesterday been filled with nothing but blank pages, now had not only a title and images, but the start of a story too. Charlie's story.

Charlie frowned as he read through the details of everything he had lived over the past couple of days and tried to make sense of what was happening. Then the writing came to an end, and blank pages stared back at him once more. Charlie gazed down at them in disbelief.

'What on earth is happening here?' he whispered to himself. And then something else started to happen, something that Charlie would never in a million years have believed if he wasn't seeing it happen with his very own eyes. There, on the blank page, another image began to appear. It started slowly, just a line or two at first, followed by more lines and details. Charlie could do nothing but watch, somewhat afraid, totally mesmerised, and completely incapable of tearing his eyes away from what was appearing. He watched as streets appeared, and shops and trees. He saw a field and an abbey and roads and lanes come to life on a page that had been blank just seconds before. Eventually the image, drawn piece by piece before him in the same deep blue as the book's cover, was apparently complete. And Charlie realised he was looking down at a map. In the middle of the page, at the centre of the whole thing, was a long, snaking road. Along it, it said simply, *Crankhall Lane.* There were houses along Crankhall Lane and trees and shops, and various other, smaller streets veered off from it. At one end of the street, it narrowed into a short, thin lane that led to a field. And in the field, were the familiar ruins of a medieval abbey that Charlie had known since he was small. Along Crankhall Lane, an arrow pointed to one of the houses and a label next to the arrow read, *Charlie's House.* At various points on the map, along three other streets that were near Crankhall Lane, three other houses were pointed out by arrows. Each of these arrows was labelled, *Paige's House, George's House,* and *Sheena's House.* Charlie took a sharp intake of breath. Those were the names of his three best friends. Taking in all the details of the map, Charlie's eyes finally rested on another label. At the end of Crankhall Lane, in the field with the medieval abbey, an arrow pointed directly to a large archway at the abbey's ruined entrance.

'I know that archway,' Charlie said to himself.

Next to the arrow that pointed to the abbey's archway, in big capital letters, it read: *THE PORTAL*.

Charlie's eyes widened in disbelief. 'The portal,' he whispered, suddenly feeling excited. Charlie knew something about portals because he had once read a story book about a portal. A portal was a door that allowed people to travel to other times and places. A portal was a gateway to other worlds.

As he thought about what he was seeing and wondered what it could all mean, the page opposite the map began to give up its blankness. This time, instead of an image or a map, it was words that began to appear. Charlie watched as, letter by letter, the book began to write more of the story it wanted to tell:

Long ago in an ancient land, a boy king wandered Egyptian sands.
Too soon did he meet his fate, and for justice he has had to wait.
Throughout all of history, his death has remained a mystery,
but whilst many now, they search for proof, there were those who knew the truth.
And now we seek he who will put things right, and bring the truth into the light.
For order, chaos cannot beat, and truth, it cannot face defeat.

When the rhyme was written, Charlie turned to the next page to see if anything else would appear but it didn't.

Charlie read through the words over and over again. 'Ancient Egypt,' he said to himself. And then, as he read the words 'boy king' for what felt like the hundredth time, his eyes looked straight to those that were, as always, staring back at him from his window sill.

'The book's talking about you,' he said excitedly to the miniature death mask. 'It's talking about you and your mysterious death.'

The eyes stared back intensely. Charlie looked at the words again and then began to smile, his own eyes sparkling with excitement.

Charlie waited some more, willing the book to reveal more of its secrets. But none came. Disappointed, he sighed as his eyes caught sight of the clock on his desk and saw that it was getting late. He had been up in his room looking at the book for hours - and he still hadn't done his homework.

'It's too late to do it now,' he said to himself as he finally went to close the book, but just as he did so, the page with the rhyme flipped itself over, and something else began appearing on the next page.

You are the one, Charlie.

Charlie sat back suddenly in his chair. 'It's talking to me,' he said, in disbelief. 'What does it mean, *I'm the one?*'

You are the one who must solve this mystery.

Charlie looked around his room, unable to shake the feeling that he was being watched.

We invite you to go through the portal, Charlie.

Charlie did nothing but stare.

It's time to solve the mystery of the young King's death, the book continued, the letters appearing slowly and deliberately on the page. *The time has come for him to live in peace in the afterlife. All mysteries need a solution if those involved are to rest. You can give him that gift, Charlie.*

The writing paused, and Charlie thought it had finished, but then a final sentence appeared. *This is your path.*

Charlie sat up straight in his chair and puffed out his chest a little at the thought. He could be the one to answer the great unanswered question of how Tutankhamun died. He looked again at the death mask on his window sill and at the posters of ancient Egypt that hung on his walls, and he thought about how it would be to say yes to such an adventure as this.

Step through the portal, Charlie, and step onto your path. We have been waiting for you.

'Why me?' Charlie thought to himself, suddenly feeling uncertain again. 'Why would the book choose me?' Charlie felt his heart sink, 'I'm not clever. It would take someone clever to solve the mystery of the death of Tutankhamun.'

He sat back in his chair and looked down at his hands as his mind wandered to the abbey archway he knew so well. And then another thought came into his mind. 'I've stepped through that archway plenty of times,' he thought, 'and the only place I've ever ended up is on the grass on the other side! I haven't got a clue how to step through it into ancient Egypt!' He started to roll his eyes as he realised how silly this all was. 'This is nuts,' he said under his breath.

But then the book continued...

To activate the portal:

1. Travellers must stand before it at sunrise - not a minute later.

2. All travellers must hold on to one another if they are to arrive at the same destination.

3. As the travellers stand before the portal, they must repeat the following incantation, three times:

> *To a time that has gone before, we ask to step through Egypt's door.*
> *Egypt's boy king we wish to find, and an answer we seek to how he died.*

The book finished with three final sentences. *Go prepared*, it said. *And don't go alone. The rest, Charlie, is up to you.*

The book fell silent and Charlie continued to stare at it with a mixture of excitement and disbelief. The book before him, the book that only yesterday was completely blank, was talking about solving the mystery of the death of Pharaoh Tutankhamun. And it was asking him, Charlie Swain, to be the one to do it.

CHAPTER FIVE

It was Friday morning and although Charlie loved the Friday afternoon that brought him double history, he first had to get through a morning of double Chemistry followed by double P.E. This morning, they were doing an experiment to separate salt from sand and their Chemistry teacher, Mrs Jacobs, was handing out an instruction sheet to guide them, step by step, through the process.

'Right then!' Mrs Jacobs said to the class, as she handed out the last of the instruction sheets. 'All we need to do now is mix the salt with the sand so that we can begin.'

The class watched as their teacher made a theatrical display of pouring a load of salt onto a pile of sand and mixing it all in together.

Charlie couldn't see the point. He turned to his friend, George, sat next to him at the bench. 'So we now have to do an experiment to separate the salt from the sand when it was separate from the sand to begin with?'

George turned to look at Charlie through his thick, black rimmed glasses. 'Exactly,' he said in a low whisper so Mrs Jacobs wouldn't catch him talking in class. And then, in all seriousness, he added, 'It's called learning.'

'It's called wasting my time.' Charlie was not convinced. When would he ever need to separate salt grains from a pile of sand?

Behind them, Sheena leant forward. 'I agree,' she whispered. 'My dad once told me that salt is really good for soothing the pain of a bee sting.'

Beside her, Paige frowned. 'What's that got to do with anything?'

'Well, I'm just saying, all that salt would've been really useful to keep aside for bee and wasp stings. It's no use to anyone now it's all mixed up with the sand.'

George sighed. 'Well that's why you need to know how to separate the two, so you can get at the salt and then use it for,' he paused and rolled his eyes, 'bee stings.'

'Oh yeah, that's practical,' Sheena replied. So, the next time I'm with someone who's been stung and they're crying in pain, I'll just have to tell them to hang on whilst I get out my Bunsen Burner.' She started to wave her hands around dramatically as she spoke, 'It's ok, I can help you but I just need to get some salt out of this pile of sand first - shouldn't be more than a couple of hours.'

'Do you four have something you'd like to share?' Mrs Jacobs' voice betrayed her annoyance.

Charlie, Paige and Sheena stopped talking immediately.

'Sorry, Miss.' It was George who apologised.

'Ok then.' Mrs Jacobs pushed her glasses back up onto the bridge of her nose. 'Right, everyone can come to the front and take some of the salt and sand mixture and get started on the experiment. I'll bring around last week's homework whilst you're working.'

The class did as they were asked and each person collected a cup of sand from the front of the lab before returning to their places and lighting up Bunsen Burners.

George made sure his lab coat was done up properly and placed some goggles carefully over his glasses. He then lined up all of the apparatus he would need neatly in front of him before he began to follow the instructions with care, making sure he did exactly as they said, in the order in which they said it.

'Charlie Swain, where is your lab coat?'

'Sorry, Miss. I forgot it.'

Mrs Jacobs sighed. 'Not again, Charlie,' she said as she pulled a spare from a box in the corner of the room. 'Honestly, you'd forget your head if it wasn't screwed on.'

Charlie smiled sheepishly and took the offered lab coat. 'Thanks, Miss.'

George handed Charlie a pair of goggles without looking up from his work.

'Thanks, George.'

Twenty minutes later, Charlie was quite enjoying himself. He had successfully poured water into the sand and salt mixture and swirled it around to ensure the salt had dissolved into the water. He had allowed the sand to settle to the bottom of the beaker and was now pouring the water, which contained the dissolved salt, into another container.

'And what are you going to do next?' asked Mrs Jacobs as she passed by Charlie's seat.

'I'm going to heat it, Miss.'

'Excellent! And why are you going to heat it?'

Charlie looked over at George. 'Erm...' He thought for a moment, suddenly feeling a little unsure of himself. He hoped he had this right. 'I'm going to heat it so the water will evaporate and leave the salt behind.'

He looked at George again, hoping for reassurance.

Behind Mrs Jacobs, George nodded to confirm he was right.

'Wonderful!' Mrs Jacobs replied. 'And since you clearly know what you're doing Charlie, I will expect your written report to show that you understand.' Her voice took on a tone that was an attempt at being stern but really showed that she was fond of Charlie, even though his grades were rarely too good. 'I know I taught you last week but I'm not sure you were actually with us. You did last week's experiment with everyone else, yet your report appears to be about something else altogether!'

Mrs Jacobs dropped Charlie's work onto the bench in front of him. Glaring back from the paper was a big red D in a clumsy circle. Sat along the bench in front of him, two of the class's smartest students, Ben and Alex, turned to watch as Mrs Jacobs returned Charlie's work, before turning back around and sniggering together.

Charlie saw Paige glare at them but she had time to do nothing more as it was apparently her turn to have her work returned by Mrs Jacobs.

'Not a bad effort, Paige,' said Mrs Jacobs, her pristinely-kept lab coat rustling as she moved around the classroom. 'However, I am certain you could do better if you paid more attention to the task before you and less to what everyone else around you is doing. I've given you a B, but I think you could get higher if you would just focus more.'

Paige nodded as she turned her attention back to Alex and Ben, who were whispering and giggling amongst themselves.

'And Sheena.'

Sheena looked up at Mrs Jacobs from her seat.

'Much as I admire your artistic ability, scientific diagrams should be done using the universally accepted symbols for scientific equipment - not using your own artistic impressions of lab equipment.' Mrs Jacobs rolled her eyes and tried to conceal the small smile appearing at the corner of her mouth. 'Nor, Sheena, should they be pink.'

Paige stifled a giggle as Mrs Jacobs dropped the report in front of Sheena. She had a C.

Continuing to move around the class, Mrs Jacobs barely stopped at George's seat. 'Excellent work, as ever, George,' was all she said, as she placed his A grade report in front of him and continued to do the rounds.

*****

It was after break and Charlie, along with the rest of his class, was gathered around a starting line ready to have a go at the hurdles. Their P.E. teacher, Miss Barber, had told them last lesson that they would be trying the hurdles today but Charlie had tried to pretend it wasn't true. He was not looking forward to this. At just average height and lacking sporting ability, Charlie was sure he would never be able to jump over the hurdles. As he stood now, looking along the running track with the hurdles laid out before him, he was more certain than ever that he was right.

'I've read up on it,' George told him as he stood beside Charlie. 'There's a technique. If we follow the technique, then there's no reason we shouldn't be able to jump over them.'

'What's the technique?' Paige chimed in, moving to stand next to them. 'Sorry, I couldn't help overhearing.'

'Eavesdropping, more like,' George replied. 'You were standing five metres away!'

Paige shrugged. 'I've got good hearing. So, what's the technique?'

Taller than most people in the class, George looked down at Paige as he answered her. Paige pulled the hairband from the end of one of her blonde side plaits and re-plaited the pigtail as George offered his advice for jumping the hurdles.

'First you have to decide which leg will leave the floor and go over the hurdles first. You will most likely have one leg that naturally leads, just like most of us are naturally right or left handed.'

Charlie and Paige nodded. So far so good.

'Next, you need to know how many strides you will need to take between the starting line and hurdle. As the hurdles are spaced evenly apart, you should take the same number of strides before every hurdle. This will be different for everyone because it depends how big your strides are when you run.'

'Well how do we know how many strides we'll need to take?' asked Paige.

'Test it out now, before we start.' George began running up to the first hurdle and then ran back again. 'I just took six big strides,' he said, 'so I know I will take six strides before having to jump over the hurdle.'

Charlie and Paige both ran up to the first hurdle and back. When they got back to the starting line, George was doing some stretches. 'They say you should stretch first,' he said.

'But how do we actually make it over the hurdle?' asked Paige.

'When you get to it, jump with your lead leg forward to go over the hurdle first, then bend your back leg up behind you and sweep it sideways over the hurdle whilst you're in the air.'

'Then what?' The concern in Charlie's voice was reflected by the worried look on his face.

George shrugged. 'Then do it all again and again until you reach the finish line. If you follow the rules, everything should work out.'

Charlie raised his eyebrows. At a good head and shoulders taller, George, Charlie reckoned, had a much better chance of jumping those hurdles than he did.

Miss Barber blew a whistle. 'Ok everyone, line up please, ready to start.'

Most people were already more or less at the starting line, but a few stragglers took their time walking over and Miss Barber blew the whistle again. 'Come on!' Charlie thought her shout was louder than the whistle. 'We haven't got all day!'

Charlie stood sandwiched between George, who was on the outside lane, and Paige. Sheena made her way over to stand with the group.

'Ok. Focus,' said Miss Barber, offering her advice. 'All you've got to do is make it from one end of the track to the other.'

Sheena stood with her hands on her hips looking down the track. 'I reckon I can do that.'

Charlie admired her confidence. 'I wouldn't be too sure.'

Sheena smiled. 'Miss Barber has just said that all we've got to do is get from one end of the track to the other, right?'

Charlie nodded, a grimace appearing on his face at the thought of what was about to happen.

'That's easy,' said Sheena. 'Watch and learn.'

Miss Barber blew the whistle again. 'Ok, get yourselves ready. You will go on the next whistle.'

The class got themselves into position.

'Ready...steady...go!'

The whistle blew and everyone in the class began to sprint towards the first of their hurdles.

Paige reached the first hurdle before anyone else and from way behind her, Charlie watched as she vaulted it like a pro. Yet watching Paige didn't give him any more confidence and as the hurdle approached, he closed his eyes and leapt into the air. Seconds later he felt the sting of a knee grazed against gravel and the pain of his hands sliding along the floor. The hurdle was tangled in his feet.

Miss Barber had seen what had happened but wasn't about to let him get out of it. She blew the whistle again. 'Come on, Charlie! Get up! Keep going!'

Charlie struggled to his feet, blood running from his knee, and saw Sheena ahead of him, happily ducking beneath the hurdles.

'This is the hurdles, not limbo dancing, Sheena!' Miss Barber yelled.

Charlie struggled to his feet and started running again. As he reached the next hurdle he kept his eyes open, deciding that if he fell again, he would be able use all his senses to help himself. This time he didn't fall - but he didn't leap high enough either. Instead, the hurdle fell down behind him but he kept going. He leapt over hurdle after hurdle, knocking each one to the ground. 'Will this ever be over?' he thought to himself as he gritted his teeth and attempted to jump over the last hurdle along the track. Finally, he reached the finish line to the sneers of Ben and Alex who, as well as being smart, were also, somewhat unfairly, good at sport. Charlie realised, with disappointment, that they seemed to be good at everything.

'Looks like you're as rubbish at sport as you are at science!' Ben jeered.

'It's not just sport and science,' Alex joined in, 'his grades are terrible in everything!'

'Why do you even bother trying, Charlie boy?' said Ben, through his laughter. 'You really are rubbish.'

Suddenly, Ben's demeanour changed and the look of enjoyment on his face was replaced with pain. 'Ow!' he shouted as he felt his arm being twisted behind his back. He squirmed. 'Let me go!'

'I'll let you go when you've learnt to stop being so spiteful!' Paige's blonde plaits swung around as she fought to keep hold of Ben's arm. 'I think you need to apologise to Charlie.'

'What for?' said Alex, still smirking. 'Ben was only speaking the truth.'

'Oh really?' Paige tightened her grip on Ben's arm and pushed it further up his back. 'Your friend isn't doing much to help your case, is he?' she said to him.

'Ow! Ok, ok. I'm sorry!'

Paige let go of Ben's arm and pushed him away from her, a look of rage on her face.

Charlie was too astounded to speak.

'Wow, Paige! That was fantastic!' said Sheena with enthusiasm. 'Remind me never to upset *you*!'

'Come on, George!' Miss Barber's voice let them know that, in the commotion, they had missed the fact that George had still not made it to the finish line. They looked back all the way to the first hurdle where George, determined to perfect the correct technique, was still trying to make it over. Each time he tried and failed, he simply went back to the start line and tried again. Every time he tried to jump the hurdle, he knocked it over, just as Charlie had done.

'Looks like you're not the only one who's rubbish at sport, Charlie,' said Alex.

Ben laughed at Alex's comment, momentarily forgetting what had just occurred.

Paige took an angry step towards them and both stepped backwards, their hands held up in surrender. Ben stopped smiling and rubbed his arm.

'Oh, for heaven's sake!' Miss Barber shouted. 'Just walk around them George! The lesson will soon be over!'

The whole class watched as George, still determined to jump at least one hurdle properly, tried one more time. Two grazed knees and elbows later, he admitted defeat and walked slowly towards the finish line.

When he finally arrived, he was greeted by Sheena talking excitedly. 'You should've just run under them like I did!'

George looked at her disapprovingly. 'Hurdles are designed to be jumped over, not run under.'

Sheena was unfazed. 'Says who? Anyway, if you'd have done it my way you wouldn't have missed everything.'

'Why? What did I miss?'

'You missed loads!' Sheena waved her hands around dramatically as she began to tell George a story that was somewhat more exaggerated than the one that had actually taken place. 'Ben and Alex were picking on Charlie, so Paige beat them up!'

'Don't exaggerate!' Paige shook her head as Sheena spoke but she had a smile on her face that said she was pleased with herself.

'I'm not!' Sheena looked at George, who raised his eyebrows questioningly. 'Honestly, George, I'm not!'

George looked to Charlie, who agreed with Paige. 'You are exaggerating, Sheena!' He said, laughing. 'Paige was brilliant though!'

'Why can't you just tell the story like it was?' George asked Sheena.

'Why can't you just break the rules occasionally? If you'd have spent your time trying to make it to the finish line rather than trying to do everything exactly right, you'd have seen it for yourself, and then there would've been no need to hear my version of events, would there?'

Charlie watched George and Sheena bickering before him, and he looked over to Paige who had stood up for him just a short time ago. As he looked at his friends he thought about the book and knew with absolute certainty that it was no accident it had labelled the homes of his three friends on the map. These were the ones the book wanted him to take through the portal. He smiled to himself. In reality, whatever the book said, he would never choose anyone else.

CHAPTER SIX

It was lunchtime and Charlie, George, Paige and Sheena were all sitting huddled around a table in the corner of the dining hall. They were talking in hushed voices so that no one else could hear.

'What kind of adventure?' Sheena was wide eyed.

Charlie wondered how best to explain it. 'Perhaps it will make more sense if I just show you.' Charlie looked around to make sure no one was paying any attention to them before pulling the book from his bag and placing it in the middle of the table.

The others looked at Charlie questioningly.

'Open it,' was all Charlie said.

George pulled the book towards him and lifted the front cover, as Paige and Sheena leant in to look at it with him.

Charlie watched their faces as they read. One by one they finished reading what was written.

'I don't understand,' said Paige. 'You're telling us that the story in this book is what actually happened to you on Wednesday afternoon?'

'Yes.' Charlie nodded in agreement as Paige looked at the others.

'So,' said Sheena, sounding uncertain, 'you're telling us that an alleyway just appeared at the top of Crankhall Lane?'

'Charlie nodded again.

'With a book shop in it?' added Paige.

'Exactly,' said Charlie.

George said nothing but was listening intently to every word. Charlie couldn't decide if he was listening so hard because he was genuinely interested in the contents of the book or because he was trying to work out whether Charlie was out of his mind.

'And the book was blank?' Paige asked, looking at Sheena from the corner of her eye.

'Completely blank,' agreed Charlie.

'And all this,' Sheena pointed at the book, 'just...*appeared*?'

Charlie nodded emphatically. 'Yes,' he said. 'That's what I'm telling you. And look,' he continued, desperate to convince them of all that had happened, 'the map even has your houses marked on it. I think it wants us all to go through the portal together.'

Sheena and Paige shared the same look of confusion. 'And the portal is the abbey archway, the archway in the field at the bottom of Crankhall Lane?' asked Sheena.

Charlie was losing patience. 'Yes.'

'And you think we have to go through it to solve the mystery of the death of Tutankhamun?' Sheena continued. 'We have to go back to ancient Egypt?'

Charlie sighed and leant back in his chair, feeling annoyed.

Paige and Sheena studied him intently, before looking at each other and then, expectantly, at George.

George leant forward further and tried to help them. 'Why would an alley and a bookshop suddenly appear?' he asked.

Charlie's shoulders dropped a little. 'I don't know why. The man in the shop said it was a pop up shop - that it would only be around for a short time and then it would move on.'

George nodded slowly. 'I've heard of pop up shops,' he said. 'But you're saying this one *disappeared*?'

This time Charlie didn't say anything. Instead he only sighed.

'And the abbey archway, the archway we've all walked through a thousand times, is somehow a portal that will take us to ancient Egypt?' asked George.

'According to the book, yes.'

'Then how come we've never found ourselves stepping through the archway into somewhere other than the field at the end of Crankhall Lane?' asked George.

Charlie sighed again, more deeply this time. 'Because,' he said, pointing to the book and feeling increasingly annoyed, 'you have to step through at sunrise and say the -' Charlie stopped in his tracks as he heard the words he was about to speak and realised how crazy they sounded. He sighed again and spoke quietly, suddenly feeling silly, '- the incantation,' he said, finishing the sentence.

The others said nothing more but all three of them studied him with interest.

'Oh, look,' said Charlie, feeling as annoyed with himself and with the book as he did with his friends. 'If you don't want to believe me, that's fine. I'll find someone who will.' Charlie stood up and reached behind him to pick up his bag, aware that he too would find this difficult to believe if he hadn't experienced it for himself.

'Charlie,' said Paige as he got to his feet.

'Just forget it, Paige.'

'Charlie,' she said a second time.

There was something in the tone of her voice that made Charlie stop and look at her. In his annoyance, he hadn't noticed the book's pages flip quickly over until they reached the next blank one. Unlike Charlie, the others had seen it, and all six eyes were locked on the book, waiting to see what would happen next.

Charlie looked behind him to make sure no one else was near and remained standing to conceal what was going on at the table.

'It's, it's...' Sheena managed, pointing at the book and unable to finish her sentence.

'I know it is,' breathed Paige, without breaking her own stare.

'I can't believe this,' whispered George, his brow crumpled into a deep frown that displayed his confusion.

'I told you,' said Charlie, feeling relieved that he no longer had to convince them.

There, right in front of them all, the next blank page of the book began to display words. One by one the letters appeared as they asked a simple question. *Wouldn't you like an adventure?*

George looked at Charlie and then back at the book, and then back at Charlie. He kept opening his mouth to speak but nothing came out. The others were struggling with the same problem.

In the end, Charlie broke the silence. 'I told you it was real!' he said, a little more loudly than he had intended. And then, dropping his voice to no more than a whisper, he said 'I'm thinking of going to test out the portal. Who wants to come with me?'

All three of them stared at Charlie in total disbelief, and still not one of them uttered a word.

Finally, Paige spoke. 'This book,' she said, pointing down at it with a look of complete confusion, '*and you*, want us all to go through a portal to solve the mystery of the death of Tutankhamun?'

Charlie nodded, 'Yes.'

'To ancient Egypt?'

Charlie nodded again.

'To see Tutankhamun?' she repeated.

'Well, to find out how he died, yes.'

'I can't believe this!' In her excitement, Sheena was a little louder than she had meant to be and a few people at neighbouring tables looked around.

'Shhhh,' said Charlie, placing his finger across his lips. 'No one else can know.'

George still looked stunned. He kept looking at Charlie and back to the book.

'Why is it so important to find out how Tutankhamun died?' Paige asked.

'Who cares?' said Sheena, her enthusiasm growing. 'This is a real adventure!'

Charlie smiled. 'The book says Tutankhamun can't live in peace in the afterlife because no one has ever told the truth about how he died. But,' he continued, 'Sheena's right. Wouldn't you like to find out for yourselves? And to see ancient Egypt with your own eyes?' Charlie felt his heart leap with excitement. 'Wouldn't you all like to come with me?' he asked. 'Like the book said, wouldn't you like an adventure?'

'Hang on a minute,' said Paige, tilting her head to one side and frowning. 'That could take ages! How will we be able to spend days or weeks, or even longer, away from home without anyone missing us?'

Charlie looked disappointed. 'I hadn't thought of that,' he said. 'You're right Paige. Perhaps we can't go after all.'

'Look!' said Sheena, pointing excitedly at the book. 'It's saying something else.'

The other three looked back at the book and saw that Sheena was right.

Time is but an illusion. It said. *When you go through the portal, it will be as if time in your world is standing still. You could be gone for years and you will still return on the same day that you left. There is nothing to fear.*

Charlie looked from the book to the faces of his friends. Paige was a picture of disbelief, Sheena looked genuinely excited, and George looked completely shocked.

'What do you say?' Charlie whispered. 'Would you like to go on an adventure back to ancient Egypt? Do you want to be the ones to find out how Tutankhamun died?' He paused and then dropped his voice so that it was even quieter. 'Do you want to come with me through the portal?'

All three stared back at Charlie and then looked at each other.

'Absolutely!' said George, finally breaking the silence. His eyes flashed with excitement. 'We have got to do this!'

*****

The clock said half past two and that meant Charlie was about to have what was to him the lesson of the week. He entered his history classroom and sat down contentedly in his usual seat. As was the case in so many other lessons, it was George who sat next to him but he hadn't arrived yet - George's English class obviously hadn't finished on time. Charlie leant back in his chair and smiled to himself. English class had just finished, the weekend was just an hour and twenty minutes away, his favourite lesson was about to start, and when he got home tonight he would be gathering together everything he needed to go through the portal. He and his friends planned to leave first thing tomorrow morning. Charlie couldn't wait.

The classroom door flung open and Ben and Alex, followed by the others who were in the top group for English, came into the classroom. As Alex passed Charlie's desk he tripped and dropped the books and pens he was carrying all over the floor.

'Clumsy!' said Ben, laughing at his friend's misfortune as he pushed past him and headed for the back row. Charlie bent down and picked up a book that had landed next to his feet, and then handed it to Ben. Ben took the offered book but gave no word of thanks as he rushed to join Alex at the back of the room.

George took his seat next to Charlie just as their history teacher, Mr Cook arrived. 'That was a nice thing you did, handing Alex's book to him,' whispered George. 'I'd have let him pick it up himself. He didn't even thank you for it.'

Charlie shrugged. 'Alex and Ben just don't like me,' he replied quietly, looking down at his desk.

'I wouldn't let it worry you,' whispered George. 'I don't much like *them*.'

'Good afternoon, class!' Mr Cook finished arranging some papers on his desk and greeted them enthusiastically. 'Today we're going to start a new project and you will need to work in groups of four to do it. In your groups, you will need to choose an event from history and put together a presentation to tell the rest of us about it. You can present your work as a poster or a PowerPoint presentation, and everyone in the group must speak when you present to the rest of us. You will have the next two history classes to complete this project, and you will present your work to the rest of the class three weeks from today.'

A ripple of excitement ran around the room and Charlie heard some of his classmates whisper 'yes!' to their friends - everyone loved doing group work.

'Are there any questions?' Mr Cook asked, the tone in his voice making it clear that he knew he was about to be asked lots of them.

'Sir?'

'Yes, Sheena?'

'Sir, can we choose our own groups?'

'Yes. As long as the groups are made up of four people.'

From their seats at a table on the opposite side of the room, Sheena and Paige looked over to Charlie and George, who nodded back to them in agreement that the four of them should work together.

'How long do we have to do this, Sir?' asked someone sat near the back of the class.

'As I have just told you, you will have the next two history lessons, as well as homework time to do this.'

'So what do we do, Sir?' asked someone else.

'What do you mean, what do you do?'

'What have we got to do, Sir?'

Mr Cook sighed. 'You have to choose an event from history to find out about. You will then need to present your findings back to the rest of us. You can make a poster, or a PowerPoint presentation, and everyone must speak when you do your presentation.'

'Can we do a poster, Sir?'

Mr Cook sighed again, more deeply this time. 'Yes, you can do a poster.'

'Sir?' Charlie thrust his hand up into the air with great enthusiasm.

Mr Cook looked cautiously in Charlie's direction. 'Yes, Charlie?'

'Can we do absolutely any event from history?'

'Yes,' Mr Cook nodded. 'You can.'

Charlie threw his arm upwards again.

'Yes, Charlie?'

'Sir, can our group...' he glanced at the others - they all knew what he was going to say, '...do the death of Tutankhamun?'

Mr Cook shot an annoyed glance at a few sniggers coming from the back of the room before he answered. 'That sounds very interesting, Charlie but please make sure it is factual and not filled with stories like your recent essay on ancient Rome.'

'But Sir, my essays aren't stories!'

Mr Cook looked Charlie straight in the eye. 'Charlie, your essay made it seem as though you were saying you had spoken face to face with a Roman soldier. Now, you cannot possibly be telling me that you have spoken directly to a soldier of ancient Rome.'

'No, Sir,' admitted Charlie, feeling upset that his favourite teacher hadn't liked the latest essay he had written for his favourite subject. 'But,' he said, feeling brighter, 'maybe I can get some really good information for our Tutankhamun project!'

In the seat next to him, George, apparently afraid that Charlie would say too much, kicked him in the shin.

'Ow!' Charlie exclaimed, as George's shoe made contact with his leg.

Mr Cook watched Charlie jump in his seat and raised his eyebrows. 'I have said before, Charlie that you are probably the most enthusiastic person in this class, and your passion for history is a great thing, but please ensure your facts are right. History is all about the evidence.'

'Sir?' A voice spoke from amongst the sniggers at the back and Charlie heard it whisper, 'What does he know about ancient Egypt?'

Charlie ignored the comment. 'If only they knew,' he thought.

'Yes?' Mr Cook still looked annoyed with the boys at the back of the room.

'Can we be a group of six?' Ben pointed to himself, Alex, and four others, all sat together along the back of the classroom.

'No. Like I said, you need to work in groups of four.'

The back row groaned in disappointment and Paige turned around in her seat to look at them. Ben caught her eye as she did so and he immediately lowered his gaze and rubbed his arm.

The room became quiet and Mr Cook seemed to breathe a sigh of relief. 'Right, is that everything?'

'Sir?' Another hand went up. 'Sir how long do we have to do this?'

'And can we do a poster, Sir?' another voice asked.

Mr Cook hung his head dramatically and then picked up a board marker and walked around his desk to the board on the back wall. 'I'm going to write this down for you, as you seem to be having some difficulty,' he said, obviously trying to control his annoyance. And Mr Cook, in writing that for some reason appeared bigger and less neat than usual, wrote his instructions on the board in blue pen.

'Ok. That should make everything clear,' said Mr Cook as he sat down at his desk. 'Now, get yourselves into your groups and decide on an event you would like to find out more about. I'll come around and see each group individually.'

Everyone began to stand up, to move chairs and tables, and to talk excitedly to one another about their ideas.

Then, amongst the instant noise and chaos, another voice shouted above the din. 'Sir? Sir, is it ok to do a poster?'

Sat at his desk Mr Cook didn't respond but instead dropped his forehead down towards the table until it made contact with the surface of his desk. 'Yes,' he said, his voice muffled against the desk top. 'You can do a poster.'

CHAPTER SEVEN

'Sorry I'm late!' Sheena said as she reached them. She handed Charlie her bag to hold and bent over, trying to catch her breath, 'My dad almost caught me putting food and his camping lantern into my backpack.'

'Did you tell him you were coming to mine, like we said?' Paige asked.

Sheena nodded. 'Yes,' she said, standing up straight again. 'Did you tell your parents you'll be at mine?'

'Yes. I said I'd call when I got to your house so I'll need to ring in a minute, otherwise my mom will get suspicious.'

'I need to do the same.'

'Us too,' said Charlie, handing Sheena's bag back to her now she seemed able to breathe again.

They stood by the post box at the far end of Crankhall Lane. It was a good place to meet - far enough away from Charlie's house that his mom wouldn't see him but near enough to the location of the portal. One by one they made their phone calls home. None of them lived very far away and ever since they had made the transition to secondary school, their parents had been allowing them to go alone to their friends' houses, so long as they called to say they had arrived in one piece.

'They might regret the decision to let us make our own way to each other's houses,' Paige said, smiling mischievously. 'I really don't think any of our parents would like it if they knew just where we're going!'

'I know mine wouldn't!' George responded and then, turning to Charlie, 'What's the plan now?'

'Does everyone have everything they said they'd bring?' Charlie asked his friends and, one by one, they nodded that they did. 'Ok, then,' said Charlie. 'Follow me.'

The little group did as they were asked. They walked silently, in single file, behind Charlie as he led them towards the far end of his street, where it narrowed, first into a small lane, and then into little more than a dirt track.

'Watch your footing,' Charlie warned them. 'It can get muddy down here, and the ground's uneven.'

The others looked down, being careful about where they put their feet.

Just a few minutes later the group found themselves at the very end of Crankhall Lane, looking out into a field they all knew well. In it stood the last few remains of a medieval abbey.

'There it is,' said Charlie, pointing his finger into the field.

They all looked at the field before them. A few stone walls of varying heights emerged from the long grass, and a spiral staircase, missing its top steps, wrapped around and opened out onto nothing. Nearby, gravestones sheltered by a few tall yew trees looked up from the ground and towards the sky. A large, Gothic archway, once the abbey's main entrance, was the only part of the building that still stood complete; the rest of the abbey's stones lay scattered across the ground.

'I still can't believe that's a portal,' said Paige, looking uncertain. 'That archway has always been there - and we've walked through it loads of times.' Paige marched over to the archway and stepped through from one side to the other and then back again. 'See?' she asked, opening her arms as she spoke. 'I've walked through it and I'm pretty sure I'm still here. Unless ancient Egypt is nothing like I expected it to be.'

Charlie had still not taken his eyes from the archway. He couldn't believe he was going through a portal, and to ancient Egypt, no less.

'It's not that simple, Paige. Remember, the book said we need to recite the incantation. Also, it won't work until sunrise.'

Paige looked disappointed.

Beside them, George smiled. 'Of course!' he said, in realisation. 'The word portal comes from the Latin *porta*, meaning gateway. And the portal is just that - a gateway to the past. It's logical that the portal itself would be in some physical gate or doorway. This makes perfect sense!'

'Look,' said Charlie, 'let's get everything set up, and then we can go back through everything we need to know.'

The others did as he suggested and placed their backpacks on the ground. George pulled a small sheet of tarpaulin from his bag and lay it out on the grass, ready for Charlie's tent to be set up.

Half an hour later, the friends had put up the tent, laid out their sleeping bags, and were now sitting in a circle on a blanket Paige had brought, with Sheena's dad's camping lantern in the middle of them. It wasn't yet dark but it was dusk, and the lantern brought a welcome glow.

Sheena delved into her bag and brought out boxes of juice for everyone, followed by endless containers of food. Every time they thought she had finished, she pulled something else edible from her bag.

Paige laughed at her, 'How much can you fit into one bag?' she joked, helping herself to a sandwich.

'You do know some of that will probably go off over night because it's quite warm?'

Sheena looked at George. 'Will you please relax, George?'

George leant forward, 'I'm just saying that if we want anything to eat before we go in the morning, then we might have a problem if it stays warm overnight and we have nowhere cool to put the food.'

'Here, George,' Sheena said playfully as she handed him a sandwich and a packet of crisps. 'Put some food in your mouth and stop talking.'

George snatched the offered food good naturedly and unwrapped the sandwiches, biting into them hungrily.

'Now we're all set up,' Charlie began, 'I'm going to remind you all of the details.'

The others fell silent as Charlie reminded them of everything the book had said. 'Remember, we need to say the incantation three times to get through the portal to the right time in history. We also have to be at the portal itself at the right time of the day. It's only active at sunrise.'

George immediately took out his phone and started looking something up. 'Sunrise is at 6:30 tomorrow morning.'

'That means we have to be ready and standing at the archway just before that time. The book said we shouldn't be late, and if we miss it we'll have to do all this again tomorrow night.'

'We should probably try and get some sleep then,' said George as he finished the last of his crisps.

'I don't think I've got much chance of going to sleep,' Sheena said to her friends.

'Me either,' said Paige 'but I suppose it makes sense to try.'

'Let's set an alarm for 5am, that will give us plenty of time to put our things away and be ready,' said Charlie.

'Let's all set our alarms,' George suggested. 'Just in case.'

They all took out their phones and set the alarms to 5am before climbing into the tent and into their sleeping bags, all laid out side by side. Sheena placed the camping lantern on the ground above her head.

'No matter what, I would have been so excited to be going through the portal,' Charlie said, stifling a yawn. 'But it's even better that I know I'm going through it with all of you.'

From their sleeping bags the others smiled and Sheena reached out to turn off the light. Each one of them knew they should try to get some sleep but instead of closing their eyes, they stared out into the darkness and thought about the archway that stood outside their tent. Whatever happened tomorrow, they all knew there was an adventure awaiting them that was beyond their wildest dreams. In the face of such knowledge, sleep seemed impossible. And dreaming seemed pointless.

CHAPTER EIGHT

'It's almost time.' George looked at his watch as he spoke. 'It's quarter past six.'

Unable to stop thinking about the adventure before them, none had managed to get much sleep. Instead, they had talked excitedly until the early hours of the morning, finally drifting off just a few hours before all four alarms went off at the same time and shot them from their sleep. Yet they were all too excited to focus on being tired.

'Will the tent be ok behind that wall?' Paige asked Charlie. They had taken down the tent as soon as they awoke and Paige had placed it behind a portion of the abbey wall that amounted to little more than a pile of stones.

'It'll be fine,' Charlie assured her. 'Few people come here anyway.'

'Are you sure we shouldn't take it with us?' Paige asked.

'It's too much to carry,' said George. 'And anyway, we'll already stand out, we don't need anything else that would draw attention to us.'

Sheena finished packing away the rest of the food in her backpack. 'Does anyone want anything to eat?'

'I've told you - that might not be safe to eat anymore. It was warm last night, and it's going to be really hot where we're going.' George responded.

Sheena took a bite of something triangular and pastry encrusted and intentionally looked at George as she bit into it. 'Taste's fine to me.'

'What's that?' asked Paige.

'It's a samosa,' Sheena replied, as a pea fell onto the grass.

'For breakfast?' George asked, incredulous.

Sheena shrugged. 'It's tasty. Does anyone else want one?'

Everyone shook their heads. George, it seemed, had already decided he wasn't going to risk eating food that had gone through a warm night without the benefit of a fridge. Charlie and Paige were too excited to eat.

Charlie looked at Sheena, happily eating her breakfast. 'There's just one more thing to do,' he said.

The others watched as Charlie went into his bag and pulled out a piece of paper.

'What's that?' asked Paige.

'I wrote down the incantation for us to say. It seemed easier than trying to hold the book or worse, remember it.'

'Here,' he said to Paige. 'I did two copies. You have the other one.'

Paige took the paper. 'So what now?' she asked.

'How long to sunrise, George?' Charlie asked his friend.

George looked at the brightening sky and then down at his watch. 'One minute.'

'Everyone line up and hold hands,' said Charlie, remembering that the book had said they should all hold on to one another.

Everyone did as they were asked, and now Charlie, George, Sheena and Paige stood holding hands, and standing staring through the abbey archway.

'What happens next?' asked Paige.

'Just wait,' replied Charlie. 'At sunrise, we all say the incantation three times.'

The friends stood staring intently at the archway as Charlie suddenly felt something like panic. 'What are we doing?' he thought to himself. 'We're about to travel a very long way, to a time we don't know.' Charlie began to wonder whether they should be doing this at all but before he had time to offer his thoughts, George spoke.

'Twenty seconds, Charlie,' George updated them.

'Do you have the incantation, Paige?' asked Charlie.

'Yes,' she replied. Charlie stood at one end of the row, holding Sheena's hand in one of his own, and holding the incantation in the other so that both he and Sheena could see it. George held onto Sheena's other hand, and at the far end of the row was Paige, with the other copy of the incantation. She held the incantation in her right hand, and gripped George's hand in her left.

'Make sure everyone is holding on to each other's hands tightly!' shouted Charlie, still feeling nervous and uncertain. 'We don't want to lose anyone.'

'Don't say that!' said Sheena, gripping his hand so tightly it hurt.

George informed them there were just ten seconds to go.

'Get ready,' said Charlie. 'Right on sunrise, we start chanting the incantation three times, then wait to see what happens. When the time is right, we step through the archway. Stick together, hold on to each other, and don't hesitate.' Charlie sounded more in control than he felt.

They all fixed their eyes on the archway, waiting to see what would happen. At first, all they could see was the usual, empty arch standing in the dawn light. It looked eerie but otherwise appeared just as it always did.

Beyond the archway, the tip of the sun just touched the horizon, its orange glow spreading fiery tendrils out across the morning sky.

'Say hello to Amun-Ra,' said Charlie. 'It's sunrise. Chant now!'

They all did as they were asked.

'To a time that has gone before, we ask to step through Egypt's door. Egypt's boy king we wish to find, and an answer we seek to how he died.'

They chanted it together in perfect rhythm, once, twice and then for a third and final time. For a few seconds, nothing changed. All they could see was the usual archway with the grass beyond.

And then it happened. It appeared as a fine shimmer at first, a slight glitter within the archway that was barely noticeable. Then it intensified. The four friends watched in amazement as the shimmer and glitter became a whirling mass of sparkling fog and mist. It swirled, thick and energetic, for a few seconds but then it began to slow down and clear slightly, and through it they could make out shapes. The shapes appeared as vague shadows at first but then the outlines became more vivid. Images of stone circles, followed by great pyramids whizzed past their eyes within the mist. They watched, mesmerised, as impressions of Spartan warriors were replaced by those of Roman emperors, and as a shadowy vision of a Greek temple was quickly replaced by a Roman amphitheatre. They squinted their eyes to make sense of what they were seeing as the sparkling mist showed them shadowy outlines of battlegrounds where soldiers fought one another, first with swords and lances, and then with cannons and guns. Images of Viking ships gave way to a vision of a battlefield where a king was thrown from his horse by an arrow that flew dangerously close to his eye, and crowds of women marching through the streets with banners and signs were replaced with what looked like bombs falling from planes, themselves replaced in the mist by tanks driving through a desert. They watched, awe struck, as scene after scene of human history played out before their eyes, making them feel dizzy. And then it stopped. The scenes flying by in front of them came to an end, and instead the mist cleared completely. Without the mist, the archway seemed filled with a shiny, glass-like substance, and now, instead of scenes from history, the archway showed them a very different image. Before them, they watched as four friends, two boys and two girls, appeared and looked back at them from the archway. Charlie, George, Sheena and Paige were looking back at themselves. Yet they were not prepared for what happened next. From within the archway, their reflections looked back at them - and then waved, before beckoning to them, their hands slowly and silently calling them forwards.

'Now!' shouted Charlie, and without hesitation, all four stepped forward.

Had anyone been in the field to see this, they would have watched, dumbfounded, as four children stepped through an apparently empty archway and, piece by piece, disappeared into it. First their leading feet and legs, followed by their heads and shoulders and the rest of them, leaving, for just a second, only their back legs and feet behind them. Then they too stepped through the archway and disappeared. And all that remained was the usual abbey archway, rising from the uncut grass, and a tent hidden behind a small, ruined wall. If anyone had watched what had happened, they would never have believed their eyes.

CHAPTER NINE

'Ow!' Charlie sat up and rubbed his arm as he watched George, Paige and Sheena scatter on the floor around him. He hadn't been prepared for how fast and violent travel through the portal would be. 'Is everyone ok?'

'I think so,' said George, adjusting his glasses that now lay diagonally across his face.

Paige clambered to her feet looking slightly bewildered and offered a hand out to help Sheena. 'We're fine.'

Charlie and George also stood and brushed the dust from their trousers with their hands.

The group looked around them. They were surrounded on all sides by tall, lush, green plants. Before them a large lake, framed with reeds and rushes, stood serenely in the baking heat, its still surface dotted with pinkish-white flowers that floated on the water. Above them the sun burned in a perfectly clear sky.

'Are you sure this is ancient Egypt, Charlie?' asked Paige, looking uncertain. 'I thought ancient Egypt was full of pyramids and temples, not trees and lakes.'

Charlie heard the question but he didn't look at Paige. Instead his eyes were drinking in the scene around them. 'I've seen pictures in books that looked like this,' he said, almost whispering in awe. 'But I never thought ancient Egypt would be this beautiful.'

'Did you know it would be this hot?' asked Sheena, pulling her long, dark hair behind her neck and tying it back. 'It's boiling!'

'What did you expect?' asked George. 'We're in Africa, not the Arctic.'

'I was just saying,' replied Sheena, good naturedly.

'Look!' said Paige, pointing just above the lake, 'What kind of bird is that?'

The others looked in the direction of Paige's pointing finger and watched as a large bird with a white body and black head, tail and legs landed by the lake. It bent its head downwards and dipped its long, curved black beak into the water.

'I've never seen anything like it,' said Sheena.

'It's an ibis,' said George.

'A what?' asked Paige.

'An ibis,' said Charlie, agreeing with George. 'They were, or rather are,' he said, correcting himself as he remembered where they were, 'sacred to the ancient Egyptians.'

The ibis withdrew its beak from the lake and gazed intently into the water. Then it suddenly plunged its head back in and just as quickly pulled it back out again, this time with a fish in its beak. Then it flew away, its large wings spanning outwards.

'Why are they sacred?' asked Paige.

'They're associated with the god Thoth,' Charlie answered.

'I've heard of Thoth,' replied Paige, frowning as she tried to remember. 'Wasn't he the god of writing?'

'That's right,' agreed Charlie. 'And the god of wisdom.'

They watched as the bird flew out of sight, and then they continued to look around them. There was so much to take in.

'We need to remember this place and wherever we go from here, we have to remember how to get back. That's how we'll get back home,' said George pointing to an archway behind them. 'That's the archway we came through.'

At George's words, Charlie froze.

'What's the matter, Charlie?' asked Paige.

But Charlie couldn't speak. He was suddenly filled with fear.

'Charlie,' said George. 'What is it?'

Charlie could see his three friends staring at him, awaiting his answer, and he forced himself to speak. 'The incantation,' he said, his voice filled with panic. 'The incantation that brought us here.'

'What about it?' asked Sheena, a confused frown on her face.

'I never thought about getting home again.'

The three others looked at Charlie in silence, as they tried to understand what he was saying.

In the end, it was George who spoke. 'You mean there's no incantation to get home?'

Charlie watched as Paige and Sheena looked at George in horror, and then turned their attention back to him.

'No, that can't be it,' said Sheena, smiling at Charlie encouragingly. A few seconds later she sounded less certain, 'That's not it, is it Charlie?'

Charlie swallowed.

'Charlie,' said Paige, the tone in her voice a clear warning that she would not be impressed if George were right.

Charlie nodded slowly. 'There's nothing in the book about an incantation to get home.'

'What?' said Paige, her voice low and menacing.

Charlie grimaced. 'I'm sorry, I was just so caught up in everything that I didn't think...'

Sheena put her hand to her mouth as George sat down hard on the ground.

'We've come here without any way of getting back again?' Paige's eyes were on fire. 'I can't believe this!'

'I'm so sorry,' said Charlie. 'I -'

'Oh, my life!' said Paige, putting both hands on her head and looking up towards the sky.

'Calm down, Paige,' said George.

'Calm down?' shrieked Paige. 'Calm down? We're in ancient Egypt - *ancient Egypt George* - and we have no way to get home again!'

'I know where we are,' said George. 'But panicking isn't going to help us.'

Paige glared at him.

'He's right, Paige,' added Sheena. 'And it wasn't just Charlie - none of us thought about how to get home. We were all so wrapped up in everything else, that we forgot the most important thing.'

Paige dropped her shoulders, and fell onto the ground next to George. 'I suppose you're right,' she said. 'I'm sorry, Charlie.'

Charlie hung his head a little. 'I knew I wasn't clever enough for this,' he thought to himself. And then he looked to his left, where Sheena stood sniffing and trying not to cry.

'Don't worry, Sheena,' he said, reaching out a hand to put on her arm. 'It will be ok.'

'How?' asked Sheena. 'I can't believe we forgot about getting home. What if we're stuck here? What if I never get to see my family again?'

Charlie felt a pang at the thought of never again seeing his mom or his grandad or his auntie Mariam. He tried desperately to think of something to make himself and his friends feel better. 'The book gave us the incantation to get here,' he said. 'Maybe it will give us an incantation to get home?'

'Of course!' said George, jumping to his feet. 'The book! Look at the book, Charlie. Let's see if there's anything new in it. Maybe there'll be an incantation for getting home now that we've arrived?'

Charlie pulled the book from his bag as his three frightened friends gathered around him. 'There's more writing,' he said, feeling hopeful.

'What does it say?' said Paige, who had softened her voice again.

Charlie looked. The book had added to the story. It told of how they had camped out by the portal, and how they had stepped through it at sunrise. It told of how they were surrounded by plants and birds and a lake, and how Charlie had realised there was no incantation to get them home.

'Does it tell us how to get back?' asked Sheena eagerly.

Charlie shook his head and read them the last sentence in the book. 'When all is said and done, a hero is nothing if he does not believe.'

'What does that mean?' asked Paige. 'Believe in what?'

'Perhaps it means we have to believe we will find the incantation to get home,' suggested George.

'Well that's just great,' said Paige, sarcastically.

Sheena looked at Paige. 'We didn't believe Charlie about the book and the portal until we saw it for ourselves,' she said. 'But it was all true. The book got us here, and I believe it will get us home again.'

George nodded in agreement. 'It's our only hope.'

Charlie agreed. 'The book has answered us,' he said. 'It's told us what we have to do. We just have to believe in the book.'

Paige sighed. 'I suppose there's not much else we *can* do. But,' she said, pointing over at the archway, 'one way or another, I'm going back home through that portal!'

The group all turned to stand before the archway they had fallen through just minutes before. This archway was different from the one back in Crankhall Lane. Unlike the curved and somewhat pointed arch of the abbey entrance, this one was formed by two square pillars with a flat stone across the top. Each pillar was painted a golden yellow colour and stood on a square base that was painted blue. The top of each pillar was brightly decorated with a pattern that looked like feathers, or perhaps flower petals, reaching upwards. The stone across the top was painted in the same golden yellow as the pillars. Flowers were painted across its centre and at each end, a blue eye looked back at them. The eye was outlined, also in blue, and a straight blue line came out from beneath it. A longer line, ending in a swirl, flowed beside the straight one.

'The Eye of Horus,' Charlie said, staring at the image. Then he turned to the others, enjoying himself as he told them what he knew. 'Horus is the sky god and has the head of a falcon. That's why the Eye of Horus has those lines underneath it - they're meant to show the markings on a falcon.' He pointed up towards the eyes looking down at them from the archway. 'The Egyptians believe the pharaoh is Horus in human form, and that the Eye of Horus protects both the pharaoh and his people. The eye is also a symbol of the power of the pharaoh.'

 The Eye of Horus

They all stood staring up at the archway. It didn't appear to be attached to any further room or building but instead rose up from amongst the foliage. On either side of the archway were two tall palm trees that were laden with clusters of some kind of fruit.

'They don't look much like coconuts,' said Sheena.

'They're not, that's why,' replied George.

'But aren't they palm trees?' asked Sheena, looking a little confused.

George nodded. 'Yes, but not all palm trees are coconut palms.' He nodded his head in the direction of the trees. 'They're date palms. The fruit you can see hanging down are dates.'

'Oh cool,' said Sheena, as she looked around her feet and picked up a stone.

'What are you doing?' asked George.

'Getting something to eat,' replied Sheena.

'You've only just eaten.'

'Travelling makes me hungry.'

'You've only stepped through an archway! You literally finished your breakfast a few minutes ago.'

'I'm in ancient Egypt, George. I think you'll find that means I have travelled a very long way and it's been several thousand years since I have eaten.'

'Technically,' said George 'the fact that you're in the past means you haven't even been born yet, and that means you've yet to eat anything at all.'

Sheena gave George a victorious look. 'Well either way, I'd be very hungry then. Either I've never eaten anything or I haven't eaten for thousands of years. Whichever way, I think I deserve something to eat.'

George shook his head in exasperation and watched as Sheena made her way over to the date palm and started throwing the stone she had found up towards the fruit.

'Sheena, don't do that!' George whispered with urgency. 'We don't know where we are - you could draw attention to us!'

Sheena ignored him and kept throwing the stone. 'There's no one around here, George. You can see we're alone! Anyway, I'm nearly there.'

'Sheena...'

'Ok, ok, it's done now.' They all watched as a few ripe dates rained down from the palm leaves, landing on the ground around the tree's trunk. Sheena gathered them up and dropped them into a plastic bag she fished out of her backpack. 'We don't know how long we're going to be here. Extra food could come in handy.' She smiled, proud of herself. 'Does anyone want to try one?'

Paige took up Sheena's offer and bit into a date. 'Ow!' she said in surprise.

'Dates have stones in them,' said George, giving up on trying to reason with Sheena and helping himself to a date. 'They're tasty - really sweet.'

Charlie joined the others in tasting the fruit and then Sheena put the bag of dates into her backpack. 'We need to gather any extra food when we can.'

George nodded to show he realised she had a point. 'Just try not to be so noisy about it. We don't know what risks we face.'

Sheena didn't respond to George's request but instead asked a question. 'So where do you think we are?'

The group of four looked around them again.

'There's a path,' Paige informed them as they all turned to look in the same direction. 'Perhaps we should follow that and see where it leads?'

'That seems like the best idea,' said Charlie, feeling his earlier fear give way to excitement about what lay ahead. 'Who knows what we'll find at the end of it!'

They all began to follow the path as it wound around the side of the lake and out through the trees and lush foliage ahead of them.

'Don't forget to pay attention to your surroundings,' George reminded them, 'If we want to get home again, we need to be able to find our way back to this archway.'

The others did their best to pay attention.

'Quick, this way!' Charlie whispered to them, and George and Sheena followed him into a clump of heavily scented jasmine bushes.

'What's wrong?' asked Paige. 'Why are you all in the bushes?' She stood looking at them from the path, her hands on her hips.

'Just step in here, Paige,' Charlie pleaded.

'But why? What's going on?'

'Do you have to answer everything with a question?' asked George, 'Can't you just trust us?'

'I do trust you,' Paige replied, still standing on the path. 'I just like to know why I'm doing something, that's all.'

'Well, would you like us to explain it to you from behind these plants, or whilst you stand on the path in full view of those guards over there? The ones with the spears and the daggers!'

George looked from Paige and back in the direction of the guards, who were just visible through the leaves and branches. They stood, tall and stony faced, on either side of a large porch in a grand looking brick building that was painted white.

Paige looked in the same direction as the others, out towards the guards in the distance.

The two men wore white, pleated, skirt-like garments that came down past their knees. Their necks and the tops of their arms were circled in thick, gold jewellery, and on their heads, they wore some sort of soft head covering that was white. Behind them, the porch walls and ceiling were covered in brightly painted tiles that decorated the porch in swirls and flowers. In the back wall of the porch, was a doorway in front of which two more guards stood. They held their spears upright, the sharp and dangerous tips glinting in the Egyptian sun.

Paige stood still, staring forwards, her mouth hanging open, 'Oh, my...'

'Oh, for heaven's sake!' George suddenly reached out his hand and pulled Paige off the path and into the bushes with the rest of them.

'Ouch!' exclaimed Paige, in surprise.

'Really, Paige. One of these days your inquisitiveness is going to get you into trouble. Can't you just act first and ask questions later?' whispered Sheena.

'Sorry,' Paige responded, a little sulkily. 'I just like to know what's going on.'

They all fell quiet as they looked at what lay ahead.

'I'm beginning to think this was all one big mistake,' said Paige, recovering from her mood.

'I know what you mean,' said George. 'Those spears look really sharp.'

'Maybe we should just go back the other way,' suggested Sheena, sounding afraid. 'We need to get as far away from those guards as possible.'

'There was no other way,' said Charlie.

'Maybe we should just go back to the lake and wait for sunrise?' suggested Paige. 'Maybe the book will give us the incantation to get home and we can just go back to where it's safe.'

'We can't just leave!' whispered Charlie. 'We're in ancient Egypt! There's so much to see!'

'We won't see anything if we're on the end of a spear!' said Paige.

'Maybe Paige is right, Charlie. Maybe we should just head back to the portal and wait for the next sunrise,' added Sheena.

George nodded. 'I think we're in real danger here,' he said, his face clearly showing his concern.

Charlie watched as the girls nodded in agreement and all three of them looked at him expectantly.

'Let's just go back,' said Paige. 'We can say we've stood in ancient Egypt now. The rest we can read about.'

'Have you forgotten why we came?' asked Charlie. 'The book said we have to discover the truth about the death of Tutankhamun so he can rest in peace. We can't just leave!'

'What if the book's not on our side?' asked George. 'For all we know it could be leading us to our own deaths!'

'The book said we have to believe,' said Charlie. 'And I choose to believe in the book. You can go and wait for sunrise if you want to, but I'm going to carry on.' Charlie tried, rather successfully, to hide the fear that his friends might take him up on the offer and he would end up alone.

The others looked at Charlie's determined expression and one by one they agreed to stay.

'Well, if one of us is going, we're all going,' said Paige.

Charlie felt a rush of relief. He needed his friends.

Sheena nodded. 'We'll be safer together than split up.'

'Agreed,' sighed George.

Resigned to the fact that they were not going home just yet, the others went back to looking through the bushes.

Out in the distance, beyond the guards and the white building in front of them, there was flowing water. Charlie squinted his eyes to see better against the brightness of the sun. 'Look,' he told the others, 'there's a river over there.'

The others all looked past the building and saw that Charlie was right. Out in the distance, a wide river carried boats along it and passed by impressive temples and other buildings that stood on the opposite bank.

'And that's not just any river,' said Charlie, suddenly realising what he was seeing. His eyes gleamed with excitement. 'That's the Nile.'

Sheena's eyes grew wide. 'Don't they have crocodiles in the River Nile?'

'Yes,' nodded Charlie. 'And hippos.'

'Look over there,' said George, his finger pointing through the leaves and branches to a temple on the other side of the river. 'Does that look like Luxor Temple to you, Charlie? I did some reading before we came, and it looks like Luxor Temple to me.'

Charlie looked, doing his best to remember all the details of the poster he had on his wall of that very building. 'Yes,' he said, turning to George and feeling sure of himself. 'That's definitely Luxor Temple.'

Charlie took his backpack from his shoulder and knelt down next to it on the floor. The others watched as he removed a piece of paper from his bag, unfolded it, and then lay it out on the ground, holding down the corners with stones. At their feet, Charlie had laid out a map. 'Here's the Nile,' said Charlie, tracing the river with his finger, 'and here is Luxor Temple. The temple was in the main area of the city - the city centre, if you like.'

'You thought to bring a map?' asked George.

Charlie nodded. 'I printed it off the computer. I thought it might be useful.'

'That's really clever thinking,' said Paige, and Charlie felt a hint of pride.

'Why didn't I think of that?' said George, clearly irritated that such a sensible thing hadn't been his idea.

'Why does it say Thebes on the map?' asked Sheena.

'Because the place we call Luxor was called Thebes by the ancient Greeks,' Charlie told her. 'So maps of ancient Egypt often call it Thebes - even though the ancient Egyptians themselves actually called it Waset.'

'So we are really in Waset?' asked Sheena.

'Exactly,' said Charlie. 'And we're not far from the city centre and this temple.' He pointed again at Luxor Temple on the map.

'Well that's great!' Sheena said, sounding optimistic. 'At least we know where we are!'

'And if we want to find out as much as we can about Tutankhamun, and about Egypt during his reign, it would make sense to go to the main area of the city,' said Paige.

Charlie nodded in agreement.

'So, we're here?' asked George, pointing out their location on the map. 'And the Temple is there,' he said, moving his finger, and looking at his friends expectantly.

'So, what's the problem?' asked Paige, looking from George and then back through the jasmine towards the guards and the white building and the river. 'The river looks huge from here,' she commented.

'It really does,' said George, beginning to lose patience.

'And we're not even right by it,' added Paige.

'No,' said George. 'We're not.'

Sheena looked back out towards the river and nodded, agreeing with Paige.

'Hang on!' Paige exclaimed. Her face looked concerned.

George raised his eyebrows expectantly.

'That's the river there, right?' she asked, pointing to the river on the map.

'That's the Nile, yes,' agreed George.

'And that's the temple, there?'

'Yes.'

'But that means...'

George sighed.

'What?' asked Sheena, frowning.

'Oh, dear,' said Paige looking at the others. 'It means we're going to have to get across the river. We're on the wrong side!'

'Yes - and no,' said Charlie, a knowing smile on his face.

The others looked at him expectantly.

'At some point we're going to have to cross the river, just like George says,' said Charlie. 'But we aren't necessarily on the wrong side.'

'What do you mean?' asked Paige. 'Either we're on the wrong side, or we're not.'

'Eventually, we surely need to be over there,' said George, sounding sure of himself as he pointed at Luxor Temple on the map again.

'We already know that,' said Paige, growing impatient.

'Yes,' agreed Charlie. 'But at the moment, we're here.' Charlie placed his finger on a point on the map and waited whilst the others huddled closely around to look.

'But that's...' Sheena's voice trailed off as she looked at the map.

'Exactly,' said Charlie. 'That's the royal palace. That,' he continued, standing to his feet to look again at the white building through the trees, 'is the palace of the Pharaoh.'

CHAPTER TEN

Sometime later, Charlie, George, Sheena and Paige were still hiding in the jasmine bushes and looking across at the guards standing in front of the white building.

''I'm still worried about how we're going to get across the river,' said George.

'So am I,' replied Charlie. 'But we've got bigger problems at the moment. Before we even think about crossing the river, we have to think about how we're going to get into the palace. And before we can do that, we need to distract those guards. Otherwise we'll find ourselves skewered on the end of those spears like a pig ready to roast.'

As they peered through the leaves and wondered what to do, Charlie, Paige and George suddenly became aware of a crunching noise behind them. They all turned around and saw Sheena, standing back a little and munching her way through a bag of crisps. They looked at her in disbelief.

'Sheena, what are you doing?' George shook his head as he asked the question.

'You talking about a roast pig made me hungry,' she replied, speaking through a mouthful of salt and vinegar crisps. 'Does anyone want some?' she asked. 'I've got plenty more in my bag.'

The others stared at her and then George turned back to look through the trees, saying nothing. The expression on his face said it all.

Charlie joined him in looking back at the palace, realising that finding a way in would be difficult.

Paige turned to Sheena. 'What other flavours have you got?'

Sheena smiled and took her back pack from her back. 'Every flavour,' she said. 'What would you like?'

A moment later and Paige had joined Sheena in having a snack. 'I hadn't realised how hungry I was,' she told the others. 'I'm starving!'

'Well just make sure not to leave any litter behind - we don't want anyone to know we're here,' ordered George. 'And when we come out from behind these bushes, you can't have anything else, you'll make too much noise.'

Sheena and Paige happily finished off their snacks.

'That's given me an idea,' said Sheena.

'What has?' asked Charlie.

'Noise,' answered Sheena. 'We need to make a noise, over there,' she said, pointing past the guards. 'If they think there's someone on that side of the building, won't they go to investigate?'

'Probably,' said Charlie, unable to contain his excitement at the thought of walking through the Pharaoh's palace. 'Let's try it!' he said, enthusiastically.

'There are four guards though,' said George. 'Do you think all four will go and investigate?'

'Who knows?' said Sheena, shrugging her shoulders. 'Has anyone got a better suggestion?'

The four friends looked around at each other. No one had any other idea of how they could get past the four frightening looking guards.

'Ok then,' said George. 'But how will we do it?'

Paige's face lit up as George asked the question. 'I've got it!' she said. And now it was Paige's turn to slide her back pack off her shoulders and delve into her bag. She rummaged around inside it. 'Where is it?' she said under her breath. 'I know it's in here somewhere.'

The others watched as she scrambled through the items in her bag for what seemed like ages, before she finally found what she was looking for.

'Found it!' said Paige, looking pleased with herself, and she pulled from her bag a bright, yellow tennis ball.

'A tennis ball,' said Sheena, sounding underwhelmed.

'Why have you got a tennis ball?' asked Charlie, sharing Sheena's uncertainty.

'Surely you didn't think we'd have time for a quick game of tennis?' asked George.

'I always keep a tennis ball in my bag. Playing with a tennis ball helps me to think.'

'So you're going to sit behind these bushes with the tennis ball, and *think*?' asked Sheena, frowning. 'I don't think that's much of a solution, Paige.'

Paige sighed. 'I'm going to throw the ball over there to distract them.' The others looked in the direction she was pointing. 'Look at the guards,' she continued. 'Those standing inside the porch, on either side of the door, can't see as much as the other two because they're surrounded by the walls and ceiling. The two guards standing on the outside, on either side of the porch entrance, keep looking both to their left and their right to make sure they're looking everywhere and don't miss anything. All we have to do is get over there,' she said, pointing towards a clump of tall, green leaves on the opposite side of the building. 'Then we wait until they're both looking away from us - and then I will throw this ball to the right hand side of them. With any luck, they'll think there's someone on that side of the building and they'll go and look, leaving this side of the building and the entranceway free of guards for a moment or two.'

The others thought about Paige's suggestion. If anyone in their little group could aim well and throw a ball far enough, it was Paige.

'What does everyone think?' asked Paige.

The others looked at each other and then nodded.

'I think Paige can do it,' said Charlie.

'So do I,' agreed George. 'But what if all the guards don't go and investigate?'

Paige shrugged. 'If it doesn't work we'll have to think of something else - but it's got to be worth a try.'

'Ok, Paige,' said Charlie. 'Let's try it!'

'Follow me,' Paige responded, clearly enjoying being in charge. 'Keep close.'

The others did as they were asked and followed Paige as she crept, close to the ground, behind the rows and clumps of trees and plants until they finally arrived at their destination.

'Now what?' asked Sheena.

'Now we wait,' said Paige. 'We wait until both of those guards at the front of the porch are looking back over there.' Paige pointed back in the direction of the jasmine bushes they had first hidden behind.

The four friends watched intently as the guards looked around them.

Paige had to wait until her moment came. 'Come on! Look that way,' she whispered, willing both guards to look in the right direction at the same time. And then, finally, it happened.

'Now, Paige!' said Charlie, a little too enthusiastically.

From their hiding place, Paige threw the tennis ball as hard as she could past the entranceway and along the side of the building, and the friends watched as the two guards looked at one another questioningly. The guards from inside the porch had obviously heard the noise too, and they stepped forward to speak with the others. A short time later and the two guards from the front of the porch had run around the side of the building in the direction of Paige's tennis ball. The other two guards had run off around the other side of the palace, presumably to catch anyone trying to run in the opposite direction.

'Quick!' said Paige. 'There's not much time!' And she began to run towards the palace entrance, with Charlie, Sheena and George close behind.

They ran fast, past rows of trees, through the white-washed archway, into the brightly painted porch and through the doorway to the royal palace. Once they had made it through the door, they immediately moved to stand between the wall and a huge, painted column that stretched from the floor all the way to the ceiling. Here they stood still, leaning up against the wall, catching their breath.

When they had recovered, they all looked approvingly at Paige and then took a moment to look around them. To their left, on the other side of the doorway through which they had come, was a column identical to the one they now hid behind. Both columns were huge and towered imposingly above them. Both were wide but they grew even wider at the top and were painted to make it look like flower petals reaching up towards the ceiling. The rest of each column was painted in broad stripes of bright red and blue. These were the only two columns they could see. The rest of the long, thin space opened up before them and felt more like a corridor than a room. Its floor was covered in tiles that were painted with yellow swirls on a blue background. Above them, the ceiling was covered in white flowers edged in blue. The walls had nature scenes on them and they could see birds, like the one they had seen at the lake, standing in amongst reeds and near water.

They all stood, looking up at the ceiling and the columns, and staring in disbelief at the decoration on the walls around them.

'It's amazing,' said Charlie. He spoke in a low whisper but the empty room still filled with the echo of his voice and the group knew they had to move on.

'Those guards will be back any minute,' said George. 'It's not safe to stay here.'

'We have no choice but to keep going that way,' said Charlie, pointing forwards and away from the entrance. 'But we'll have to be quick - there are no more columns to hide behind, and we don't want to be seen.'

As Charlie finished speaking they heard a noise outside the doorway that told them the guards were back at their posts.

Charlie put his finger to his lips to tell the others to be quiet and then he waved with his hand to show they should follow him. They did as he asked and soon they were walking slowly sideways, their backs to the side walls, as they tried to make their way silently to the other end of the room. Finally, they made it and they passed through another doorway that brought them to a large room, decorated just as brightly as the last one. Four columns formed a square in one of the far corners of the room but otherwise, the room was empty.

'This is fantastic!' Charlie said loudly.

'Shhhh!' said the others together, afraid that someone might hear.

'There's no one here!' said Charlie. 'Look at this place! Isn't it amazing?'

'Shhh,' said George again. 'It is amazing but it won't be amazing if we get arrested by the royal guards.'

'Or worse,' said Sheena, shivering at the thought.

'I can't wait to tell Mr Cook about this!' said Charlie. 'He'll never believe it!'

'He definitely won't believe it,' said Paige. 'He'll just keep telling you to stick to the facts rather than tell stories.'

Charlie felt disappointed but knew that Paige was right. Mr Cook was always telling him to be less inventive with his history homework but he just couldn't help it. Every time Charlie read about something that happened in the past, or looked at the posters on his bedroom wall, his mind filled with stories and images that fired his imagination. 'You're right,' he said to Paige, hanging his head a little. 'My head's always in the clouds.' Charlie felt unhappy with himself as he spoke the words. 'I wish I was smarter,' he thought to himself.

Paige's look was one of sympathy, which somehow made Charlie feel even worse. 'I like your stories,' she said. 'But you can't tell Mr Cook about this Charlie - you don't want anyone else to know about the portal. Then it wouldn't be our secret, would it?'

Charlie cheered up at the thought. 'You're right Paige! No one else gets to step back into the past and see history for themselves.'

'What's that noise?' asked Sheena suddenly, a look of panic on her face.

The others stopped to listen and they too could hear a sort of scuffling noise coming from the direction of the columns at the other end of the room.

'Isn't that the doorway past those columns?' asked Paige quietly.

'It looks like it,' answered Charlie.

'Well I, for one, am not going through there until I know what that noise is.'

'Shhhh,' said Charlie. 'We need to be quiet.'

'And get ready to run,' added George.

'Run where?' asked Sheena, her voice giving away that she was afraid.

'We'll have to go back,' said George.

'But the guards are back that way.'

'I know. But there may be some more heading towards us.'

Sheena stood frozen to the spot. The others, too, were unable to move. They stood with their eyes fixed on the four columns in front of them, wondering what was about to come out.

Suddenly there was a loud screeching noise and the sound of a vase breaking as something hurtled towards them from the shadows.

They all screamed and began to run back towards the entrance, only calming down when Charlie realised what it was that had scared them. 'It's ok,' he said, trying to breathe again. 'Look.'

George started to laugh in relief as he saw the culprit.

Paige had her hand on her chest, willing her heart to slow down.

'It's a cat!' exclaimed Sheena, as she walked towards it. 'Actually, it's really just a kitten.'

The cat eyed Sheena suspiciously at first and then, apparently deciding she was a friend, allowed her to stroke its grey, mottled fur. The kitten began to purr as it enjoyed being made a fuss of, and it rubbed its head against Sheena's leg.

'Hello,' Sheena said to it, and it gazed back at her with big, green eyes that looked out from a grey face with black stripes.

Just as they had all begun to relax a little, they heard another sound behind them. This sound was louder and more definite, and they all realised with horror that they were hearing the sound of footsteps marching with purpose through the room behind them, making their way to where they now stood.

'We have to get out of here!' whispered George. 'Quick, go through the doorway - past those columns!'

They all ran as fast as they could towards the doorway and found themselves in another corridor with no columns to hide behind.

'We can't stay here,' whispered Charlie. The sound of the footsteps was still close behind them. 'Keep going!'

They ran again, along the corridor and through another doorway. This time, the room had two rows of columns and everyone jumped behind one of them, just as a guard entered the room. The cat had apparently followed them, and it went to sit quietly at Sheena's feet.

The guard stepped through the doorway quietly and stopped, looking and listening for any movement. He rested the end of his spear on the floor and the sound of the metal hitting the tiles echoed around the room. He waited a moment more and then took another two steps forward, before stopping again. From behind one of the columns, Charlie could see Sheena and Paige. He watched as both girls looked at each other with terrified eyes. Charlie held his breath, frightened of making even the slightest sound.

'Come on out here!' the guard shouted into the room. 'I can see you, I know you're there.'

Charlie saw Paige cover her mouth with her hand.

'Come on!' the guard shouted again and this time he banged his spear loudly on the floor again but he did it over and over again, making the room ring with the sound of metal upon tile.

As he did so, the kitten, afraid by the sudden prolonged noise, shot once more out of the shadows, screeching as it ran past the guard to let him know it did not approve of the noise he was making.

'Hmm,' said the guard, annoyed. 'I knew I heard something in here - I wish the cats would stay outside. I spend half my time investigating a noise that turns out to be nothing more than those pesky cats.' He stood for a little longer, listening, but only silence answered him, and he turned on his heels and walked back out of the room.

Charlie, Sheena, Paige and George stayed behind the columns for what seemed like forever, afraid to come out in case the guard hadn't really gone. In the end, it was Charlie who peered out first and then, certain that the guard was no longer there, he stepped out into the room. 'It's ok,' he whispered to the others, 'he's gone.'

One by one, the others slowly came out from behind the columns and joined Charlie in the centre of the room.

'I thought cats were supposed to be sacred to the Egyptians,' said Paige.

'They are,' replied Charlie. 'It looks like we've found the only ancient Egyptian who doesn't like them.'

'Well then, we should be especially careful of him,' whispered Sheena. 'If he has no respect for an animal that's worshipped, he'll have no problem dealing with us.'

The others nodded.

'Has anyone noticed anything strange about the language that guard was speaking?' Charlie asked them.

The others looked at one another and shrugged.

'I understood him perfectly,' said Sheena, with a shudder.

'Exactly,' replied Charlie, his excitement growing in spite of their recent scare. 'It seems we can understand ancient Egyptian!'

As they allowed this new discovery to sink in, and as they began to recover from their fright, they heard a commotion behind them but this noise was much louder than the guard had been. This was the noise of a whole crowd of people heading in their direction, all of them talking and laughing and discussing things at the top of their voices.

The four friends looked at one another in panic and then jumped back behind the columns. From there, they watched as the cat made its way quickly back into the room and huddled in the corner. Having escaped the noise of the guard, it had apparently found itself unable to escape the throng of people coming into the palace. The cat peered suspiciously out from its hiding place as large groups of people swept through the room and out into a second room beyond.

Most of the people were important looking men. They wore skirt like clothing, similar to the guards, and they all wore heavy, gold jewellery. Some walked with a staff but it seemed to be more of an accessory than something they needed to help them walk. One by one, they passed through the doorway into whatever room was next door, and then they fell quiet before bowing to someone on the other side of the door. From then on, they continued forwards but their conversation ceased. Whilst this side of the doorway was loud and busy, the other side was completely silent.

Charlie watched as a particularly large group of people entered the room and he waved at his friends to follow him. When Charlie moved, the others did the same and they weaved their way amongst the people so that they were standing in the middle of the crowd. When the large group reached the entrance to the next room, Charlie, George, Sheena and Paige bowed quietly with the rest of the people towards a man who stood at the door and then followed as he told them where to stand. Finally, the crowd stood completely still and silent, and the four friends, shorter than everyone else, found themselves surrounded by people who cast looks in their direction, clearly suspicious of these oddly dressed strangers.

From amongst the arms and legs of countless people, the little group were able to make out something of the room in which they now stood. This room was grand. The people who had entered it now lined the walls on both sides, and formed queues facing in the direction of whatever room lay beyond. Two rows of columns also ran down the length of the room. Just like in the other rooms, the columns and walls were brightly painted but this room felt different. From between the columns, statues of the gods looked down on the mortals beneath them. Charlie, George, Paige and Sheena looked up and found themselves staring at a giant statue of Anubis. The god of the underworld, with the head of a jackal, looked back at them. In one hand, he held a staff. In the other he held a strange looking cross with a loop at the top.

'What's that?' Paige whispered to Charlie, pointing at the cross.

'It's an ankh,' Charlie said quietly, his mind immediately taken back to the bookshop on Crankhall Lane. 'It's the ancient Egyptian symbol for 'life'.'

'No talking!' yelled the man at the doorway, and Paige and Charlie immediately fell quiet.

Next to them, Sheena looked up at the ceiling, which was covered in identical pictures of some sort of bird. Its hooked beak made it likely that it was a vulture. The vultures spread their wings wide across the roof above them.

Unlike the others, George was focusing on the floor. It was covered in images of captured people - enemies of Egypt - who were tied up and who were literally being trampled on by the huge crowds of people in the room.

The four stood for what seemed like forever amongst the lines of people. No matter how long they waited, no one in the room spoke or made a sound.

Sheena let out a sudden sigh and placed her bag on the floor. 'What are we waiting for?' she mouthed to the others, but they just shrugged. No one knew what was coming next but at least, for now, they were quite well hidden from the palace guards.

Sheena rolled her eyes at their response and pulled the bag of dates from her backpack. She stood up straight, leaving the open backpack at her feet, and held the bag of dates out to the others, who stared back at her in disbelief.

'Put them away!' George mouthed, trying not to make a sound.

'Why?' Sheena mouthed back, 'We've got to do something to pass the time. We've been waiting here forever.'

George didn't try to reason with her and instead gave her a look that warned her not to draw attention to them. In the end, she rolled her eyes again and dropped the bag of dates back into her backpack. She fastened the back-pack tight and placed it on her shoulder, just as the crowd began to move silently forward.

With the distraction of everything going on around them, no one had noticed the little bundle of grey and black fur that had crawled into the bag Sheena now carried on her back.

CHAPTER ELEVEN

From their place amidst the silent crowd and beneath the huge statue of Anubis, Charlie, Paige, Sheena and George felt the queues begin to move forwards.

'We're moving!' Charlie whispered, excited at the prospect.

'But where are we moving to?' asked Paige, clearly concerned about what they could face.

George, taller than the rest of them, was able to look ahead and see what awaited them. 'They're all heading towards another doorway,' he whispered. He looked around some more. 'This way!' he mouthed, and pointed the way with his hand as he moved out from the centre of the crowd and squeezed into a small gap left between the people and the wall.

The others followed and they made their way, quietly and quickly, along the wall. The lines of people glanced at them in suspicion but none of them spoke a word. Instead, all looked ahead and moved slowly forward in complete silence.

Eventually the four friends came to the end of the room, where two large columns stood either side of a small doorway. They huddled together between one of the columns and the wall, and crouched down as a group of people were allowed to step slowly through the small doorway and into the room beyond.

From behind the column the friends were able to see the next room. It was only a third of the size of the room where the people were queuing but it was definitely grander, and guards stood in each corner, protecting it.

Four huge columns stood forming a square near the centre of the room. The columns were painted gold and at about eye level, each one had a beautifully painted picture of the same man. On one column, the man was hunting with a bow and arrow, on another he was fighting enemies from his chariot. The walls showed more of the same person, riding into battle. On the ceiling was a large, red sun with long, white wings stretched out from either side. Through the columns was a gold platform with steps on either side, and all around the platform were more images of Egypt's enemies, like the ones on the floor in the room where the crowds stood waiting. The steps up to the platform were guarded by huge, golden lions and on the platform were yet more columns, but these were smaller. These gold columns supported a gold roof with cobras all along it, their hoods out to the sides. Beneath the roof was a gold chair. Its arms had lion heads on them and its legs ended in lion paws. On the back of the chair was a brightly coloured picture of a man sat on a chair next to a woman who stood and placed a hand on his arm. Above them the sun's rays shone down. The red, white, blue and green of the picture stood out boldly from the golden background.

The four of them huddled close to the column and fixed their eyes on the room beyond. George pushed his glasses back up onto his nose.

Then there was movement in the smaller room. A young man, wearing a white tunic, entered the room from a doorway at the back, and those who had been allowed to stand inside the room immediately fell to the floor, their stomachs and foreheads close to the ground. The young man walked with a stick, but unlike some of those in the crowd he appeared to be using it to help him walk. He had a slight limp, and the red, blue and gold belt that was wrapped around his waist and draped down the centre of his tunic swung a little as he walked. With care, he made his way past the lions that guarded the stairs to the platform. The golden collar about his neck matched the gold that filled the room, and the blue stones that decorated the collar were the same blue as the stripes on his white headdress, which was held in place by a gold band across his forehead. When he reached the top of the stairs, he walked beneath the golden row of cobras above his head and sat down in the gold chair, his sandal covered feet finally coming to rest. From his place on the platform he looked out into the room through dark eyes that were edged in black eyeliner.

Charlie looked excitedly at the others.

Paige's mouth fell open in disbelief. 'Is that...?' she asked, almost forgetting to whisper.

Sheena nodded, 'I think so.'

George stared in amazement.

'Yes,' said Charlie, unable to contain his excitement. 'That man is the reason we're here. That is Tutankhamun.'

The others looked back into the room.

'And it seems,' whispered George, 'that for now at least, he is still very much alive.'

'Although he is walking with a stick,' observed Charlie. 'Perhaps he's not very well.'

'Or perhaps he had an accident,' suggested Sheena.

'What kind of accident?' asked Paige.

George pointed at the paintings on the columns and the walls in answer to her question. Everywhere they were surrounded with paintings that showed Tutankhamun hunting and fighting and riding a chariot.

'It looks like being pharaoh is a dangerous business,' whispered Paige. 'He could have had a nasty accident doing any of those things.'

'Exactly,' said George.

'Although, if his bad foot is because of an illness rather than an injury, he might have never been able to do any of the things you see him doing in those pictures,' added Charlie.

'Then why would they bother to show him doing those things?' asked Sheena, quietly.

'Because he's Pharaoh.' Charlie shrugged. 'The pharaoh has to be seen as strong and powerful, not ill and weak.'

'So those pictures might just show Tutankhamun as he wants to be seen, and not how he really is?' asked George.

Charlie nodded. 'It's possible.'

'You may rise!' An older man, who had entered the room several steps behind the young Pharaoh, stood at the base of the platform and addressed the crowd. Like the Pharaoh, he wore sandals and a tunic but, unlike the King, his shaven head was uncovered and his glare was cold. The crowd stood immediately.

'Pharaoh is busy,' the older man said. 'But he will deal with as many of you as he can.' He looked sternly at two men who stood at the front of the room. 'Step forward,' he said, beckoning them with the first two fingers on his right hand, each one adorned with a heavy, gold ring.

The two men nervously did as they were told.

'Why do you come to see Pharaoh?' he demanded.

One of the men held a scroll in his hand. 'We come to seek Pharaoh's help,' he said, holding out the scroll. 'We are brothers from a noble family, and my father's tomb was recently robbed of all its riches.'

Tutankhamun leant forward in his throne, clearly interested in what was being said.

The older man took the scroll from the nobleman's hand. 'And why do you think Pharaoh can help in this matter? Many tombs are robbed.'

'Sadly, yes,' said the second man. 'But to rob a tomb is a terrible crime. A tomb is prepared to help its owner in the afterlife. To rob it is a crime against the gods.'

'This is true,' said the older man. 'But there is little to be done after the event. Thieves do not exactly make themselves known.'

'Forgive me, Vizier,' said one of the men nervously, 'but we believe we know who did it. His name is in the scroll,' he continued. 'We have come to ask Pharaoh to deal with him for this crime.'

'Vizier,' said Charlie to himself. 'I know that word.' He frowned as he tried to remember why it was important and then he remembered something his auntie Mariam had once told him. 'The vizier,' he whispered to the others, 'was the closest person to the pharaoh. He was the pharaoh's advisor.'

George looked worried. 'Well then, if I remember properly everything I read before we came, this means that that man there is Ay.'

Charlie nodded, feeling afraid. 'I think you're right George. And by all accounts, we should be careful of Ay.'

They all looked back at the older man who was now reading the scroll he had been given.

'We should be careful of Ay?' whispered Paige, as she stared without blinking.

'Yes,' answered Charlie.

'Then he's not to be trusted?' asked George.

Charlie shook his head. 'No, I don't think so.'

'What if he sees us?' asked Sheena, fear showing in her own voice, even though it was little more than a faint whisper.

'We need to be careful,' whispered George as he turned his attention back to Ay. 'Make sure no one in that room,' he nodded towards the throne room, 'sees us.'

Back in the throne room, Ay looked down at the words on the scroll and then back at the men who had given it to him.

Tutankhamun held out his hand, asking to see the scroll.

'You need not worry about this, Pharaoh. You are busy enough. I can deal with this issue.' Ay glared at the men who had come to see the King. His look was threatening.

The men looked back at him and then dropped their eyes, clearly uneasy.

'Let me see the scroll,' the young Pharaoh demanded.

Ay turned his back to the men and walked to the base of the platform. He leant in and spoke to the Pharaoh so quietly that no one but Tutankhamun could hear. He spoke to the King for a few moments, but still did not hand over the scroll.

'My vizier will deal with this issue,' Tutankhamun told the men.

The men looked disappointed but did not dare challenge the Pharaoh. Instead they bowed their heads to show their gratitude.

'You may leave,' said Ay, glaring at them. And they left.

Charlie, George, Paige and Sheena watched as person after person, small group after small group, entered the throne room to see the Pharaoh.

'If I didn't know any better, I'd say Ay was the one in charge,' commented Charlie.

'Yes. Either Tutankhamun really trusts Ay,' observed Paige, 'or he is afraid of him.'

George nodded. 'I think you're right. The question is, which is it?'

From within the throne room, Ay raised his eyes towards the doorway, looking to see how many people still remained to see the Pharaoh. And then something terrible happened. Beyond the doorway and to the side of the room that held the remaining people, Ay caught sight of four children, dressed in a way that made it clear they didn't belong there.

'Who are they?' he bellowed, looking at the four friends huddled behind the column. 'How did they get into Pharaoh's palace?' He pointed at them as he shouted, and Tutankhamun as well as those waiting to see him also turned their attention to the little group.

Charlie stood up. 'Run!' he shouted. 'This way!' And none of his friends were about to argue with him.

'Guards!' they heard Ay shout behind them as they ran as fast as they could, pushing past the remaining people and sprinting past the columns and the statues. Anubis watched silently as they ran past him, back through the rooms that had brought them into the palace. They ran through the corridors and the room where they had seen the cat and all the time they could hear the sound of guards running behind them.

'What do we do when we get back to the entrance?' yelled Charlie as they ran. 'The guards will be there!'

'We're just going to have to run for it! I don't think there's any other choice!' shouted Paige. 'We'll be running out, not in - they won't expect it. Just make sure you run fast!'

They reached the long room with the nature scenes and they could see the sunlight shining down outside the brightly painted porch.

'Don't stop,' said Charlie. 'Stick together and run as fast as you can - and don't stop when we get outside. The guards at the entrance will follow us!'

And they ran, the sound of the guards growing louder behind them. As they approached the porch they ran faster still. And suddenly they were out again in the heat of the Egyptian sun.

The guards at the entrance watched them run by but they didn't act immediately because, just as Paige had predicted, four children in strange clothes running past them was not something they were expecting. The guards chasing after the group of friends reached the guards at the porch, who were still looking bewildered.

'Don't just stand there!' Ay shouted. 'Go after them!'

And the guards, now eight of them in total, did as they were ordered, and Ay ran with them, determined to catch whoever it was that had sneaked, uninvited and unwelcome, into the royal palace.

'Quick, over here!' Charlie shouted, as he led them past fig trees and a smaller lake framed by papyrus reeds, to a courtyard ahead. 'Look!'

George, Sheena and Paige looked where Charlie was pointing. Ahead of them in the courtyard, a large, golden chariot stood gleaming in the sun. Two dark brown horses stood already attached to the chariot, suggesting that someone had either just arrived or else the chariot had been prepared for the Pharaoh or someone else from the palace to head out somewhere.

'Come on! Quick!' Charlie shouted again, panic entering his voice as the guards drew ever nearer. 'I'll untie the horses!' he shouted. 'The rest of you, get on - and someone grab the reins!' Charlie reached the chariot first and unhooked the ropes that tied the horses to a large, wooden post rising up from the floor.

Paige, followed by Sheena and George, jumped onto the chariot's platform, and then she grabbed the reins. 'Come on, Charlie!' Paige shouted. 'The guards are coming!'

Paige whipped the horses' reins in an attempt to make the chariot move but at first the horses went nowhere. She tried again, doing it harder this time, and to everyone's relief, the horses leapt forward.

'Come on, Charlie!' Sheena shouted, and George held out his hand to help Charlie jump onto the chariot just as the horses picked up speed and leapt past the guards who had arrived just too late.

'Go after them!' Ay shouted as Paige tried to make the horses go even faster, the plumes of feathers attached to their bridles blowing backwards in the wind.

Behind them, the guards rushed to find their own chariots, and Charlie, Sheena and George looked to see what the guards were doing.

'Go faster, Paige!' said Sheena. 'They're getting chariots too!' And Paige whipped the horses' reins again and again, willing them to run faster than they had ever run before.

'Which way?' shouted Paige. 'Where should we go, Charlie?'

'I'm not sure,' answered Charlie. 'What does everyone think would be best?'

'That way,' pointed George, answering quickly. 'Head for the river!'

'The river? How are we going to take a chariot across the river?' shouted Sheena.

'We're not,' yelled George, trying to make himself heard above the noise of the horses' hooves and the chariot's large, spoked wheels. 'We're going to leave the chariot!'

'Are you crazy?' shouted Sheena. 'This is our best chance of escape!'

'Our best chance is to get as far away from the palace as possible and find somewhere to hide! And we've got a better chance of doing that in the centre of the city - on the other side of the river.'

'Whatever we're going to do,' yelled Charlie, 'we need to do it quickly. I can see chariots in the distance!'

'Oh, hurry up Paige!' said Sheena. 'We need to go even faster!'

'I'm doing the best I can!' Paige shouted back. 'I've only ever ridden a horse - never a chariot!'

The chariot hurtled along, kicking up clouds of red dust as it went. The dust was becoming so thick they were having trouble seeing through it.

'I can't see the palace any more,' said Charlie.

'I can't see much of anything!' shouted Paige. 'Is that the river?'

'Yes,' said George. 'Charlie, can you see anyone behind us?'

Charlie looked through the dust behind them. He couldn't see any other chariots, but he could see clouds of dust in the distance that told him they were there.

'They're not far away,' said Charlie, and Sheena looked back too.

'We need to go over there,' George pointed in the direction of the river, 'where those boats are.'

'Ok, I'll head that way!' shouted Paige.

'No!' George responded. 'I think it's best if we leave the chariot here and run the rest of the way. We can't get too close to the boats with the chariot or the people with the boats will know we're the ones Ay is looking for!'

'I'm not sure we should stop. I can just see the chariots in the distance!' Sheena sounded afraid, but she wasn't the only one.

'Then we need to stop now! Take the chariot over there, Paige!' George shouted, as he spotted a small, brick building near the water, some way along the river from the boats.

Trusting George, Paige pulled on the horses' reins to get them to slow down and eventually she managed to bring the chariot to a stop near the building.

'Right, let's go!' said Charlie as he jumped down from the chariot.

'Where now?' asked Sheena.

'That way,' Charlie pointed towards the river as he glanced back and saw the clouds of dust growing larger behind them. 'And fast.'

'Try not to run though,' said George, setting the pace. 'If we run, people will think it's suspicious.'

They walked as fast as they could without appearing afraid, and they finally reached a cluster of boats on the river. One boat had just pulled away from the bank but another was heading back in.

'Please hurry,' Sheena said under her breath as they heard the rumble of chariots.

They stood impatiently as they watched the boat move leisurely towards the bank. The sound of the chariots grew louder.

'Come on,' said George quietly, whilst Charlie chewed nervously on his thumb nail, and Paige tapped her foot almost uncontrollably on the ground.

Finally, as the sound of the chariots grew to an almost deafening noise, the boat reached the river bank and a man climbed out. He wore a tunic and sandals and carried a scroll. Presumably he was on his way to the palace.

The four looked down nervously and tried not to catch his eye, but he paid them little attention. He was apparently too focused on what he needed to do today to be interested in a group of children, however strangely dressed, who were on their way across the river.

'Can you take us across?' Charlie asked the boatman. 'Can you take us now?'

Even in their current predicament, Charlie was astounded by the sounds coming out of his mouth. The others looked at him, clearly as astonished as he was. Charlie was speaking fluent ancient Egyptian.

The man looked at the group, frowning as he looked at their clothes and bags. 'Are you from here?' he asked.

'No,' said Paige, impatiently. And then she too looked amazed that she was speaking perfectly with this man who lived in another place and another time, and who spoke an ancient language. 'We're just visiting. Can you take us across, or not?'

Charlie saw the chariots arrive further down the river. 'Just get in!' Charlie said to them, and George and Paige followed him as he leapt onto the boat.

The boatman started to argue with them and tried to stop Sheena from stepping on. 'I have not yet agreed to take you!' he said, holding his hand up to stop Sheena. 'This is not a free service! First we must agree a price!'

'We don't have any money,' Paige said quietly to Charlie and George. 'What are we going to do?' She looked back along the river. 'They're here,' she said in panic. 'Whatever we're going to do, we need to do it fast.'

Sheena stood alone on the bank, looking terrified.

'I know!' George dived into his backpack and pulled out a torch. 'Here,' he said to the boatman. 'If you take us across the river, you can have this.'

'What is it?' the boatman asked, looking interested.

'It's magic,' replied George. 'It has a piece of the sun inside it.'

The man stared at the torch and then started to laugh. 'You say you have a piece of the sun?' he said, laughing harder. 'In that thing? You are crazy! Or you must think I am!' He stopped laughing. 'Either pay me, or get off my boat.'

In the distance, Charlie could see guards arriving at the place where they had abandoned the stolen chariot. It wouldn't be long before the guards found it and realised the four thieves couldn't have gone far. 'We have no time left, George. We have to go now.'

As Charlie spoke, George pressed the switch on the torch. It lit up brightly and the boatman closed his eyes against the glare. When he opened his eyes again, George had turned the torch back off. The man held out his hand to take the torch, but George pulled it back towards him, staring at the boatman.

'Ok, ok, I'll take you across the river,' he said as he asked for the torch again. The man waved to Sheena to step onto the boat and George handed him the torch. He pressed the button and light blared again from the end of the torch. 'Amun,' he said in awe as he waved his hand through the light. 'Ok, my friends. I'll get you safely across the river.' And with that, he began to push the boat away from the bank.

They were barely half way across when they saw the guards and Ay walking along the river bank, asking if anyone had seen the four children who had broken into the royal palace and stolen the Pharaoh's chariot. The children were now enemies of the Pharaoh, and of Egypt.

From the boat, Charlie, George, Sheena and Paige kept their heads down, hoping that the guards wouldn't see them.

'I think we've made it,' said Sheena as she watched the guards getting smaller on the other side of the river.

'I wouldn't be so sure,' replied George, as Charlie took out the map and looked for a place they would be able to hide.

CHAPTER TWELVE

Charlie looked back in the direction they had come. In the distance, he could just make out the guards walking along the river bank, speaking to passers-by and presumably asking if they had seen a group of four unusually dressed people running from the direction of the chariot they had stolen and then abandoned.

'Where to?' asked the boatman, looking at Charlie expectantly.

Charlie looked at the man and then at the others. 'Where do you think?' he asked them.

George, having spent some time studying the map with Charlie, looked up and out, across the river. 'Can you take us there?' George asked the boatman as he extended his hand to point towards a large building of endless stone columns.

'The temple?' asked the boatman.

'Yes, the temple,' George responded.

The boatman looked down at the strange object George had given him, an object that magically held a piece of the sun inside. Then, not for the first time, he looked at the clothes of the travellers and frowned.

The group of four looked back at him in turn, unsure what he was thinking.

'Of course,' said the boatman with a quick nod of his head. 'I can take you to the temple.'

Minutes later, they stepped from the boat and found themselves standing in the shadow of the temple they had first seen from the safety of the jasmine bushes in the royal palace grounds on the other side of the Nile. Towering above them, was what they knew as Luxor Temple.

Behind them, the boatman noisily negotiated another payment with some people wanting to get to the other side of the river and turned his boat around. Sheena, Paige and George looked back over their shoulders at the commotion. It was a reminder that the guards were only a short boat ride away.

Unlike the others, Charlie didn't look behind him but instead gazed in awe at the building in front of him. 'Luxor Temple,' he whispered to himself, amazed by what he was seeing.

Though they were shaken by their near escape, George, Sheena and Paige joined Charlie in looking in wonder at all that surrounded them. For a short moment, they were so absorbed in their surroundings that they forgot all that had just happened.

'Come on,' said George, returning to reality and pulling Charlie by the arm. 'We need to move.'

They all looked around them as they walked, and all that could be heard from the little group were occasional whispers of, 'Wow!' and exclamations of 'Look at that!'

'Where are you taking us, George?' asked Paige, eventually.

'Just stay close, and follow me,' answered George.

The friends walked now in complete silence, as George led the group away from the river, along the side of the temple before them, and into the depths of the city.

Everywhere was a hive of activity. Official looking men, much like those they had seen earlier at the royal palace, walked through the streets, some carrying staffs. Dark haired women wearing long, linen dresses and adorned with jewellery passed them by, some accompanied by servants. Countless stalls had been set up outside the temple, from where people tried to sell their wares. As they passed by, the four friends could see bottles of oils and perfumes, jars containing make up, and various ornaments and trinkets.

'Please! Come and see!' one of the stall holders shouted to them, and Charlie instantly began to make his way over to him. The others acted as one and grabbed his arm, pulling him back.

'We have to keep going,' said Paige.

All around them new buildings were under construction and old ones were being updated and repaired. Builders and other craftsmen shouted from somewhere up high to their colleagues working below them, their feet still firmly on the ground.

And it wasn't only humans that filled the city. As George led the group through the streets and alleyways, they passed a man leading a slow-moving donkey which carried a large basket on its back, the contents covered over with a dark cloth. In front of them, a cat leapt out from behind a stall, where a woman stood selling bread, and bounded after a frightened, grey mouse. A few geese wandered past the stall, honking and chattering and then flapping their wings and breaking out into a run as the stall holder shooed them on with a broom.

George looked above him, and then turned left into a small, side street that ran parallel with the far end of the temple. It was quieter in the side street, and for the first time they began to feel a little calmer.

'Now will you tell us where we're going, George?' asked Paige.

119

George still held the map tightly in his hand. 'We're going to Karnak,' he said, matter of factly.

'Karnak?' asked Sheena. 'What's that?'

'It's another temple,' said Charlie, looking awe struck again. 'Well, really it's a temple complex - there is more than one temple at Karnak. I've always wanted to see it,' he said excitedly. 'Let me see the map, George.'

George handed the map back to Charlie and the others gathered around it.

'So where is Karnak?' asked Paige, not sharing Charlie's enthusiasm.

'We are somewhere here,' said Charlie, pointing out the location of Luxor Temple on the map.

'Ok,' said Paige, sounding impatient. 'But where do we want to be?'

'Well, Karnak is here,' said Charlie, placing his finger on a point on the map some distance away, and further along the river.

The others stared down at the map.

Then Paige looked up at George. 'But that looks miles away!'

'It's not just down the road,' acknowledged Charlie. 'But there's a route linking Luxor Temple with Karnak. We can just follow it. If I'm right, it's not even two miles long.'

'Two miles?' asked Sheena, a look of uncertainty on her face. 'If we're going to walk for miles,' she sighed, 'I'm going to need something to eat.'

George glared back at Sheena.

'What?' she asked him, widening her eyes innocently.

'Erm, George,' Paige interrupted.

George turned his attention from Sheena to Paige.

'If we want to be at Karnak, and Karnak is on the river...'

George nodded, confirming that Paige was right so far.

'Why didn't we just get the boatman to take us to Karnak?' she said, her voice raised.

'Calm down, Paige,' said Sheena. 'Here, have a Kit-Kat.'

Paige looked down at the chocolate bar Sheena had fished from a side pocket on her bag, and then glared at Sheena before turning her attention back to George. 'Are you telling me, George Appleton-Fleming, that you have brought us miles away from where we need to be, when we could have just been dropped off at the front door?'

'But just think of everything we would've missed if we had gone straight to Karnak!' said Charlie.

Paige rolled her eyes and looked at George, who sighed dramatically before offering an explanation. 'I asked the boatman to bring us here because if the guards ask him if he's seen us and he tells them where he took us, they will come here, thinking we are somewhere near Luxor temple, when really, we'll be at Karnak.'

'Oh,' said Paige, sounding unhappy at the realisation that George had a point, and apparently uncomfortable that she was in the wrong.

George looked proud of himself.

'The problem is, we *are* somewhere near Luxor Temple,' observed Sheena, looking up at the temple's great columns and walls.

'Then we'd better move quickly,' said Charlie. 'It's this way.'

Charlie led the way eagerly as Sheena finished her chocolate bar and stuffed the wrapper into her trouser pocket. George still looked proud of his quick thinking, whilst Paige lagged a little behind, looking sheepish.

A short walk later and Charlie came to a stop. 'There!' he said, smiling. 'There it is!'

Below them, and stretching out like a snake across the landscape, was a wide and empty avenue. Along each side of it, facing each other and disappearing into the distance, were countless, huge, stone sphinxes. Their lions' paws and bodies lay upon deep, stone bases, whilst their ram heads, with curly horns, looked out in front of them, ready to watch anyone who walked along the avenue. Behind them, rows of palm trees towered up towards the sky, their trunks surrounded by lush, green plants. Alongside the trees, ensuring they had much needed water, was a man-made water channel. Beyond the channel was a stone wall that marked the line of the avenue, and it was on the top of this wall that the four friends now stood.

'We're going to have to jump,' said Charlie. 'I can't see any other way.'

'I don't know, Charlie,' said George. 'That wall's taller than any of us.'

'It's easy,' said Paige, stepping forward and looking for a way to redeem herself. 'Watch.' And with that, Paige sat down on the edge of the wall with purpose, before twisting around and lowering herself downwards. Her feet gripped against the wall's stones and her fingers held on to the top. 'See!' she shouted up to them. 'It's not such a drop from here!' Then she jumped, dropping down to the floor with a crash.

The others looked over the wall in time to see her stand up and dust herself down.

'It's not so high,' she shouted back to them. 'Who's next?'

The others looked at each other and George nervously took his hands out of his pockets. 'I'll go next,' he said, reluctantly.

A few seconds later and George was hanging onto the wall just as Paige had done.

'That's it,' said Paige. 'Now just jump.'

'I can't,' said George, in a panic. 'And I can't get back up again either.'

'Well what do you want to go back up for?' asked Paige.

George said nothing. His eyes were closed and his fingertips had turned white from holding on so tightly to the top of the wall.

'Come on, George. Just let go,' Paige encouraged him. 'You're really not that far from the ground.'

'It's far enough,' replied George, still refusing to open his eyes.

'Well you can't stay there!' yelled Paige.

'I can do what I like!' George yelled back.

Paige shook her head.

'What if we come down next, and then we can all catch George?' suggested Charlie, looking over to Sheena. 'Hang on, George. We'll come down.'

Charlie and Sheena climbed over the wall and were soon standing next to Paige. George had yet to let go of the wall.

'We're all here now, George. Jump, and we'll break your fall,' yelled Sheena.

'No,' said George. 'I can't.'

Oh, for goodness' sake,' said Paige to the others, before she shouted back up to George, trying to sound encouraging. 'You're really not that far off the ground, George.'

Paige was right. The jump hadn't been too high for any of them but as the tallest member of the group, George's feet were only about a meter off the floor.

The other three looked at each other, wondering what to do.

'Oh, no!' Paige shouted suddenly, looking over her shoulder. 'They're coming! They've found us! I've just seen the palace guards!'

Charlie and Sheena turned pale as George opened his eyes to look and, in the panic, lost his grip on the top of the wall. His fingers slipped off the stone and he fell, screaming, into the others at the bottom. Seconds later, the friends were a tangled pile of arms and legs, struggling to get to their feet and preparing themselves to run again from the guards.

'I told you it wasn't that far down,' Paige said, standing up again with her hands on her hips and smiling, looking proud of herself.

Charlie exchanged a frightened glance with Sheena, and then the colour came back to his face as he understood what Paige had done.

'You mean, you did that on purpose?' yelled George. 'You told me the guards were coming just to get me to fall?'

'Well you're on the ground again, aren't you?' answered Paige, unaffected by the look of anger on George's face.

George glared at Paige and said nothing as she handed him his glasses, that had landed on the ground as he fell.

'Now can we get going?' Paige adjusted her bag on her back and turned to look down the avenue. 'I assume it's this way?'

George looked livid and still said nothing. Instead he simply told Paige she was heading in the right direction with the tiniest nod of his head.

CHAPTER THIRTEEN

'Now this is more like it!' said Paige as they headed further away from Luxor Temple. 'This is what ancient Egypt should look like!'

'It's fantastic!' said Charlie, feeling in his element.

'So what exactly is this place?' asked Sheena, as they walked along the avenue towards Karnak, sphinxes watching their every move. She shivered, 'I don't like this feeling of being watched.'

'This is the avenue that linked the temples at Karnak with the temple at Luxor,' replied Charlie.

'But why?' asked Sheena, still staring suspiciously at the sphinxes. 'I feel like one of these could move at any minute.'

'I like them,' said Paige.

'The avenue was created for a festival that happens every year here,' Charlie told them. 'It's called the Opet festival, and during that time the Egyptians carry statues of Amun-Ra, his wife Mut, and their son, from Karnak to Luxor Temple. At the end of the festival, the powers of Amun-Ra are believed to be given to the Pharaoh, proving his own divinity and his right to be King of all Egypt.'

'So Tutankhamun will have taken part in this festival?' asked George, who seemed to have recovered from his fall.

'Yes, I think so,' said Charlie.

'So what do we know so far about Tutankhamun, then?' asked Paige. 'After all, we're here to find out how he died. Although from what I saw today, he's still alive.'

'I don't think he will be for much longer,' said George. 'He died around nineteen and he looked somewhere around that age to me. Also, I don't think the book would have brought us to the wrong time - after all, it brought us right to the royal palace at a time when lots of people had come to speak to Tutankhamun.'

The group fell quiet. 'It's sad to think he has such little time left and doesn't even know,' said Sheena.

The others nodded in agreement.

'But then,' said George, 'would you want to know?'

'That depends on whether you could do anything about it,' said Charlie. 'If he's going to die from an accident that could be avoided, or if someone could be stopped from intentionally harming him...' Charlie's voice trailed off.

The others stopped still and looked at him. 'Are you saying you think someone might be about to kill the Pharaoh?' whispered Sheena. 'Who would do that?'

Charlie looked at his friends, unsure whether to offer his theory in case they thought it was silly. 'Ay,' he said gently.

'You think Ay would kill the Pharaoh?' asked Paige.

Charlie shrugged. 'I don't know,' he said, feeling unsure of himself. 'But I know I don't trust him. Did you see how he took over and gave everyone orders today? He even told the Pharaoh what to do. Who is confident enough to think they can give the King orders?'

They started walking again and everyone looked deep in thought about what Charlie had said. Charlie felt relieved that they hadn't laughed at his idea.

'So we know that Ay might not be all he seems,' said George, thoughtfully. 'What else?'

'Well, either Tutankhamun has had some sort of accident, or else he has some illness that causes a bad foot or a bad leg - he was really leaning on that stick. And he was limping,' Paige reminded them.

'And he was shown hunting and riding a chariot and fighting in battle in paintings all over the palace,' Sheena said. 'Any one of those things could have caused an accident that led to a bad leg and foot.'

'But,' Paige reminded them, 'as Charlie told us earlier, the Pharaoh could be shown doing those things to make him seem like a great king, and not necessarily because he really does them. If he has an illness, he might not be able to do those things at all.'

'So his death could be because of an accident, possibly caused by hunting or fighting or riding a chariot, or it could be because of an illness,' clarified George.

'Or,' Charlie reminded them, 'it could be something more sinister.'

'So it could be accident, illness - or murder,' said Sheena quietly, her face showing she was afraid of the last option.

'I suppose it could be a combination of things,' said George. I read in a science book recently, that if a wound is not properly cleaned and looked after, then infection can set in. If that happens the infection can spread, causing maggots to appear in the wound and causing the area around the wound to die. It's called gangrene. If someone gets that and it's not fixed, they literally start to die whilst they're alive.'

'Ew,' said Sheena in disgust. 'That sounds horrible.'

'And painful,' said George.

'And the Egyptians couldn't heal a lot of the problems we can easily fix today,' commented Charlie.

'That's a good point,' agreed George. 'They didn't have things like antibiotics to fight infection. Someone could die in ancient Egypt from something we see in the twenty-first century as a trivial illness that is easily dealt with.'

'So Tutankhamun could have just died from natural causes?' asked Sheena.

'It's possible,' said Charlie, feeling unconvinced.

'But we should wait until we have more evidence before we form our conclusions,' George replied, wiping sweat from his forehead with the back of his arm. 'It really is hot!'

Charlie came to an abrupt halt and pointed animatedly ahead. 'Look!' he said. 'Look! It's Karnak!'

The others looked, and their mouths fell open as they saw what lay ahead. Before them, they could see two huge, white walls, with the golden points of obelisks and the tops of brightly painted columns just visible above them. The gleaming faces of the walls, covered in vivid images, stood tall in the shimmering heat, and as the friends looked closely, there appeared to be a gap between them.

'That's the entrance,' said Charlie, unable to contain himself. 'That's the entrance to Karnak!'

'Look at that!' said Paige, sharing Charlie's amazement.

'I've never seen a building so big,' said Sheena.

George didn't speak. Staring intently forward, he never once took his eyes from the building in front of them.

'I can't believe you've never seen any of this before, Charlie - given that your grandad is Egyptian,' said Sheena, smiling at Charlie's enthusiasm.

'My grandad has always said he'll take me and show me one day,' replied Charlie. 'But even if I'd seen it already, no way would it have looked like this!' Charlie looked around him. 'In the twenty first century, a lot of this is in ruins,' he said. 'We are seeing it as it really was!'

Sheena nodded. 'I still can't really believe where we are!' she replied, her excitement matching Charlie's.

'So why exactly did you decide we should go to Karnak, George?' asked Paige.

'Because it was on the map and it seemed like it could be a good place to hide and decide on our next step,' replied George.

'It's a good choice,' said Charlie. 'It's massive!'

They all walked faster now, feeling happier as they knew they would soon reach their destination and might have a chance to sit down out of the heat and the sun. They had, it seemed, left the guards far behind.

Eventually, the walls to either side of them disappeared and the sphinxes and trees led them past what looked like a large temple to their right. Ahead, to their left, a canal ran towards the river, clearly linking the temple complex with the Nile. They continued walking onwards, until they finally passed through the gap between the huge, white walls they had seen as they approached Karnak.

'I didn't think it would be so busy,' said Charlie, looking around him. 'We need to find a place to hide.'

The little group followed Charlie past white walls and painted columns and golden tipped obelisks that towered above them.

'It would be so easy to get lost here,' said Sheena.

'So make sure we stay together,' advised George.

This was a temple unlike any of them could have imagined. It was nothing like a church or a temple back home. This was a whole community. As they made their way through the complex, they could see that there was more than one temple here. Everywhere, the god Amun-Ra looked back at them, but many images and carved hieroglyphs reminded visitors that the mother goddess Mut, and the moon god Khonsu, were also honoured here. The cartouches of pharaohs could also be seen, letting everyone know who was responsible for building this magnificent place for the glory of the gods.

And the buildings they could see weren't just temples. There were living quarters and store houses too, and everywhere people milled about, carrying out their service either to the gods or to the priests. There were lots of builders and craftsmen around too. Some seemed to be repairing images but curiously, some also seemed to be chipping images off the walls.

'Why are they removing pictures from the walls?' Sheena asked Charlie, leaning in so that those doing this strange work wouldn't hear her.

'I'm not sure what's going on here,' Charlie replied quietly, 'but in ancient Egypt they often chipped away the images or the name of someone they didn't like. It was a way of erasing them from history.'

Sheena shuddered.

There's even a lake here,' said Paige, her voice breaking through the conversation.

They all followed Paige's gaze and saw in front of them a pool of brilliant blue water. Beyond it stood a small, partially ruined building. Unlike every other part of the complex, the small building appeared to have no one anywhere near it.

'There,' said Charlie, pointing at the building. 'Let's go in there.'

They headed past the lake and made their way into the small building, where four columns still stood, holding up a crumbling roof. The steps up to the building had been intentionally broken down, so that the walk up to the front entrance was uneven, and they had to watch their footing. Around the building, they could see the remains of walls and more columns, and the arms and legs and hands of what were once huge statues littered the floor.

'It looks like this place has been intentionally knocked down,' said George, as he headed inside.

'Well, it's somewhere quiet and sheltered from the sun,' said Sheena. 'And it's somewhere we can sit down and decide what to do next.'

'And at least there's no one else here,' observed George.

'That's true,' replied Sheena. 'And that means it's a good place to hide. It means we're safe.'

Paige nodded but her voice showed that she wasn't convinced. When she replied to Sheena, she did so quietly and said only three words. 'For now, perhaps.'

CHAPTER FOURTEEN

Night had fallen, and the silver light of a full moon flooded the temple. Charlie, George, Paige and Sheena hadn't left the ruined building since they entered it earlier. Instead, they had spent the day inside, away from the intense heat and from prying eyes.

Sheena pulled a water bottle from the side pocket of her bag and took a sip. 'Does anyone want anything to eat?' she asked, undoing her bag.

The others shook their heads.

Sheena sighed. 'Me either,' she said, and George looked at her in amazement.

'What?' asked Sheena. 'I'm nervous, and I can't eat when I'm nervous.'

'You've been doing a pretty good job so far,' joked George.

'Those guards are still out there somewhere,' replied Sheena, seriously. 'And I don't think they'll stop looking for the people who stole a chariot from the Pharaoh's palace.'

George nodded in response. They were all a little subdued. It had been a long day.

Charlie stood up from his seat against the side wall of the little building and peered around the open entranceway. 'There's no one out here,' he told the others, and they moved to look with him.

Outside, the whole, massive temple complex had fallen quiet. All human activity had ceased for the day and the outside space of the complex stood empty. Only the eyes of gods and pharaohs, and of priests and priestesses, looked back at them from their places on the columns and the walls. The water on the lake was eerily still and its colour had changed from a bright, sky blue to an inky black. Tiny specks of silver glistened on the surface as the water reflected the light from the stars above.

'Look at the sky,' Paige whispered, in awe. Above them the black sky was filled with a thousand silver lights.

'That's Nut,' said Charlie. His enthusiasm was contagious.

'Who?' asked Paige, frowning at the strange name.

'Nut,' repeated Charlie. 'Nut was the ancient Egyptian goddess of the sky, she was often painted as a woman arched over the world, protecting it. And her body was painted covered in stars. She was also protector of the dead.'

Paige looked up again at the sky and then back at Charlie. 'Why would the goddess of the sky be protector of the dead?'

'Because she was said to swallow the sun at night, bringing darkness to the land, and then give birth to it again in the morning, creating a new day. She protects the dead so that they too will journey safely through the underworld and be given new life.'

'How come the sky never looks like that at home?' asked Sheena, clearly impressed. 'I can only ever see one or two stars from our garden.'

'We have too much other light,' said George. 'All the street lights and lights from houses and cars make it more difficult to see a star filled sky. You'll be able to see it better if you get out of the towns and cities.'

Charlie looked down from the sky and focused his attention on the complex before him. 'Look at that temple over there,' he said. 'It's dedicated to Amun!'

'How do you know?' asked George, looking in the direction Charlie was pointing.

'Because,' said Charlie, unable to contain his elation, 'I can read it!'

'What?' asked Sheena, as she and Paige joined George in looking over at the temple.

'Oh my life, you're right!' said George, sounding excited himself. 'I can read it too!'

'Me too!' said Sheena. 'I can read hieroglyphs!'

'This is amazing!' said Paige. 'I suppose we shouldn't be surprised, given that we can also speak and understand ancient Egyptian, but this is fantastic!'

'I've always wanted to learn how to read hieroglyphs!' said Charlie, unable to keep still. 'And now I can!'

'What's that noise?' asked Paige suddenly, looking over her shoulder. 'Can you hear it? That strange, high pitched, humming sound?'

The others looked and listened, frowning at the slight noise.

Paige looked around some more and then stared down at her arm as the sound stopped. 'Ew!' she said, flicking at her arm. 'It's a mosquito!'

'Here,' said George, returning to his bag and delving into it. 'Everyone have some of this.' George handed Paige a can.

'Mosquito repellent,' she said aloud, reading the label on the can. 'You thought to bring mosquito repellent?' she asked George in disbelief.

'It's a hot country,' George replied. 'I thought we might need it.'

Paige shook her head as she removed the lid and started spraying her arms. When she had finished, she offered the can to the others, who took it gratefully.

'You think of everything, George,' said Sheena, approvingly.

'I'm going to have a closer look around in here,' said Charlie, when he had sprayed himself with mosquito repellent. Taking his phone from his bag, he turned on the torch for extra light. 'Look at all the carvings that have been removed from the columns and the walls,' he said in awe. 'Someone wanted to make sure no one knew what this place was, or who built it.'

'I think you're right,' George agreed. 'Did you see all the carvings being removed out there when we arrived?'

'Yes,' answered Charlie, 'but I couldn't see what they were originally.'

'Me either,' said George, clearly annoyed that they didn't have any more information.

'They've destroyed statues too,' said Paige, recalling the bits of statues that littered the ground outside.

From the other side of the room, Sheena ran over to her bag and took her phone from one of the pockets, before running back again. 'Look at this!' she exclaimed. 'They've missed something.'

The others made their way over to Sheena, who was crouched down, shining the light from her phone onto an unusual looking carving on a piece of stone that lay on the floor. On it, a man was seated next to a woman who seemed to be his wife, and children played at their feet. But all the people in the image looked strange. They all had unusually wide hips and long heads. Equally unusual was the sun that shone above them. Its rays, holding crosses with loops at the top of them, reached out to the people beneath.

'That's the ankh,' said Paige, remembering what Charlie had told her back at the palace. 'That cross there, with the loop at the top,' she said as she pointed it out to Sheena and George. 'It's the ancient Egyptian symbol for 'life'.'

'I'm going to take a photo,' said Sheena. 'If they meant to remove all the images, and this is one they missed, it might be useful.'

'Someone wanted this family to be given plenty of life,' commented George as he looked at the carving. 'Look how many ankhs the sun is holding out to them.'

'And someone wanted this family to have that life taken away,' said Charlie. 'Don't forget, this is a picture they seem to have missed. If they'd seen it, they would have destroyed it.'

'The question is, who are 'they'?' said Paige, just as there was a noise outside.

They all looked at one another, and Charlie and Sheena switched off their phones. George put his finger to his lips and tilted his head to listen. The others stayed completely still, holding their breaths.

At first the noise was small, little more than a scuffle that could have easily been caused by a bird or small animal. It stopped, and they began to breathe a little more easily, but then it came again. This time it grew a little louder and came a little nearer until they clearly heard the sound of stones being trampled underfoot, small pieces of broken building and statues were being crushed further into the ground as someone walked towards them. Then they heard voices.

'I have guards out searching, but I am grateful for your help, General.'

'And I am glad to give it. We cannot allow people to steal from the royal palace and go unpunished.'

Inside the building, the four children stared wide eyed at one another. Then the footsteps stopped right by the building where the little group was hiding and, unaware that they were not alone, the voices outside continued.

Charlie, standing nearest to the wall, looked in the direction of the voices and found a tiny gap between the stones. Trying to move silently, he turned around to face the wall and placed his eye slowly against the gap. After a second or two he turned his head briefly back to face the others, his hand across his mouth. Lowering his hand, he mouthed to them silently. 'It's Ay.'

They stared back at him in shock, and George placed his finger to his lips again to remind them to stay absolutely silent. They all stood completely still, the moonlight painting them silver, like statues. Charlie put his eye back to the gap in the wall.

'And how goes the campaign?' Ay asked the other man.

'It goes well,' the man replied. 'This will be another victory for Pharaoh's army - at my command, of course.'

'As always,' Ay agreed. 'The chariot that was stolen today was a gift from the last king you defeated in battle on behalf of Pharaoh.'

The two men fell silent, apparently lost in their own thoughts, but then Ay broke the silence with an angry outburst. 'All that we do for Egypt, Horemheb, and no one brings us chariots! I am Pharaoh's closest advisor and you lead the mighty Egyptian army to endless victories!' He clenched his fist as he spoke. 'It is we who run Egypt, Horemheb!'

Horemheb looked at Ay with a stony face and gave a slight but certain nod of his head.

'Look at where we are standing!' Ay continued. 'This very building,' he waved his hand in the direction of the building from which Charlie was watching them intently, 'was put here by Tutankhamun's own father, the traitor!'

Horemheb nodded his head again. His eyes remained fixed on Ay.

'Akhenaten,' Ay spat on the floor as he said the name. 'What other pharaoh would dare to erase the image of Amun, the greatest of all the gods, from our temples and deny him the right to be worshipped? What other pharaoh would decide there is only one god who can be honoured? Only one! What pharaoh of Egypt risks angering all the gods by refusing to honour them, and then goes around building temples like this one?' He pointed again to the building where the children were hiding. 'Temples to the Aten, his precious sun disc! Temples filled with pictures of Akhenaten and his family being blessed by the Aten. No god of Egypt, Horemheb, would bless the pharaoh who denied the rest of the gods!'

'I agree with you, Ay. It is we who have righted the wrongs of Tutankhamun's father, Akhenaten. It is we who have broken down his temples and chipped away all pictures of him. It is we who have made sure the images of the rightful god, Amun, have been repaired and restored.'

'Who knows what Tutankhamun would have done without our guidance?' said Ay. 'If it weren't for us, he may have continued the work of his father, who knows? If it weren't for us the temples of Amun might still be in ruins and temples to the Aten might cover the land. Tutankhamun may not even have changed his name to honour the great god Amun. He might still be calling himself Tutankhaten, as his father called him when he was born!' Ay waved his hands around to reinforce his point. 'The living image of the Aten!' said Ay, reminding Horemheb of the meaning of the name Tutankhaten. 'Who would think of such a thing? Tutankhamun - the living image of Amun - is what he should always have been called!'

'You are right,' Horemheb replied. 'Akhenaten's decision to allow worship only of the Aten angered the priests of Amun. They held such power, Ay, and they were understandably angry when that was taken from them. Almost overnight they lost the wealth, power and status they had enjoyed for generations. That anger between the priests and the Pharaoh could have turned Egypt into chaos.'

'But that didn't happen - thanks to us,' Ay reminded him. 'We restored Amun to his rightful place, and we restored his priests to theirs. It is we who gave Egypt peace and stability again. The priests owe us a lot.' Ay's look became thoughtful and he held Horemheb's gaze for a second before continuing. 'Pharaoh has no heir,' he said, rubbing his fingers against his chin. 'Perhaps it is you or I who deserve to rule after him, Horemheb?'

Horemheb said nothing at first but returned Ay's stare. 'Perhaps you are right,' he replied. He fell quiet again, as though he were deciding whether to continue. 'But Pharaoh is young. It seems unlikely we will outlive him.'

'True,' said Ay. 'Although he seems unwell lately,' he continued, his look sinister. 'He has trouble with his foot and relies more and more on his cane. Perhaps few would think it strange if his life turned out to be short?'

The two men stood quietly but their eyes remained fixed on each other.

Then there was a noise that made them both look in the direction of the small, ruined temple beside them.

'Did you hear that?' whispered Horemheb.

'Shhh,' replied Ay, placing his finger to his lips.

Inside the temple, Sheena held her hand across her mouth in shock as she caught her heel on a small piece of loose stone, sending it scuttling across the floor.

'Get ready to run,' George mouthed to the others, making no sound.

Outside the building, Ay listened closely and took a few steps towards the wall. Moving slowly, he turned to face it, staring intently forwards. Through the gap in the wall, Charlie could see Ay perfectly. He was so near. Then Ay took a final step forward, taking him so close to the wall his nose was almost touching it. And then he inclined his head, placing his eye against a gap in the stones.

Inside the temple, Charlie took a sharp intake of breath as the eye on the other side of the wall looked back into his. Ay and Charlie stood, with nothing more than a wall between them, staring back at each other.

Then, in a flash, the cold, brown iris staring at Charlie was gone, and Ay began to move, with Horemheb close behind him, towards the entrance at the back of the building.

Charlie moved away from the wall. 'Run!' he shouted to the others. 'That way!' And he started to move towards the front entrance.

The others moved quickly. Sheena, still carrying her phone, went to grab her bag with her spare hand, but the bag was still open from when she had undone it earlier to offer the others some food, and the contents threatened to spill out onto the floor.

'I've got it!' said Paige, picking up the bag and carrying it in her arms. 'Just keep running!'

They made it out of the front of the small building, just as Ay and Horemheb ran in through the back entrance.

'After them!' shouted Horemheb, and he and Ay ran after the four, who were now wanted not only because they had stolen from the Pharaoh, but because they had overheard everything Ay and Horemheb had just said to one another.

'Follow me!' yelled Charlie as they ran back past the lake and towards the huge temple before them. 'This way!'

Charlie turned to his right and they followed him into the temple, but still they didn't stop running. They went deeper and deeper into the temple, past walls and columns, through open air courtyards and through room after room, until they finally ran through a doorway that brought them to a stop and told them they could run no further.

George, Sheena and Paige bumped into Charlie as he came to a sudden stop, and the four of them stumbled into the tiny room. The room they had entered was longer than it was wide. There were no columns inside but the walls were decorated with images of a god wearing a tall hat that looked like it was made of long feathers. In front of them was a square, stone table, and on it stood four, large oil lamps, one at each corner. They were lit, and their flames cast a flickering glow onto the locked, bronze door beyond.

'We can't go any further,' said Charlie, trying to catch his breath.

Outside, the footsteps chasing them grew louder.

'Get down!' whispered Sheena. And they all rushed to crouch down behind the stone table, just as Ay and Horemheb arrived.

'They can't have gone far,' said Horemheb.

'Well they can't have escaped through there,' said Ay, glancing into the room. 'That door's locked tight.' Ay stood briefly at the threshold, looking into the room and then, apparently satisfied that it was empty, he moved on.

The four of them watched him leave and allowed themselves to breathe.

'That was close,' said George, looking around him. 'Where are we?'

'Well that god you see on the walls, with the feathers on his head, is Amun,' Charlie told him.

'And this table looks like some kind of altar,' whispered George.

Just as they were trying to work out exactly what kind of room this was, someone else entered. They saw his feet first, walking on papyrus sandals, and then, as he came to stand next to them at the back of the table, they saw the long, white, linen garment that fell from his waist almost down to his ankles. As he stood in front of them, they lifted their gaze upwards and saw a man looking back at them from eyes lined in black. His head was completely bald.

'Who dares to enter the innermost shrine in this temple of Amun?' he shouted at them. 'Who dares to enter this place and dishonour the gods?'

'Well I suppose we now know where we are,' said Paige to the others.

'Silence!' he bellowed. 'I am the High Priest of Amun, and you will speak when I say so! The noble vizier, Ay, and the great general, Horemheb, have just asked me if I had seen anyone, but I thought the temple was safe. It seems I was wrong,' he said.

He took a step forward menacingly as he shouted at them, causing Charlie to fall backwards from his crouching position and onto the cold, stone floor. As he did, the man caught sight of a pendant around Charlie's neck.

'Praise the gods!' he said, lowering his voice and moving even closer to get a good look at the pendant. 'You wear the scarab!'

None of them spoke, afraid of what might happen next.

'You wear the scarab,' he said again. 'You wear the symbol of the blessed Amun.'

Charlie instinctively reached up his hand and took hold of the pendant his auntie Mariam had sent him from Cairo. He looked down at the beetle and, for the first time, the hieroglyphs on the back of the pendant became more than just images. They became words. *May Amun always protect the wearer of this amulet*, it said.

No one spoke. Charlie let go of the pendant and it fell back against his chest. The priest stood staring at them, clearly trying to decide who they were. And then the silence was broken by a small, high pitched noise. Everyone in the room looked in the direction of the noise just in time to see a small, grey and black, fluffy head pop out of Sheena's bag, which Paige still carried. They all watched as two pointed ears stuck above the bag's rim, and two big, green eyes looked out at them.

'Bastet!' The priest took an intake of breath and stepped back, lowering his head a little in respect.

'Who's Bastet?' whispered Paige.

'The cat goddess,' Charlie whispered back. 'Don't forget, cats were sacred to the ancient Egyptians.'

'Praise be!' the priest continued as Paige looked back into the wide eyes of the cat. 'You must indeed be friends of the gods!' He looked over his shoulder as he spoke, listening to the sound of footsteps getting closer and moving with purpose towards them.

'Yes!' said George, acting quickly. 'We are friends of the gods. We have the protection of Amun and Bastet and we ask that you help them in their promise to protect us. Ay and Horemheb are trying to capture us, but if they succeed they will bring the wrath of the gods down on Egypt. If you stop them, then the gods will shower down blessings on you.'

Charlie looked at his friend in admiration, wishing he had thought to say such a thing.

The priest listened, transfixed, his eyes filled with wonder. Then Ay and Horemheb entered the room.

'We heard shouting, Wennefer,' Ay said to the priest. 'Have you found them?'

Wennefer moved to stand at the side of the stone table, offering those hiding behind it a little more protection. 'No, no,' he said. 'I stubbed my toe, that's all. It was very painful.'

Horemheb and Ay looked at him with suspicion. 'It was an awful lot of shouting just over a stubbed toe,' Horemheb commented.

'Yes, I'm sorry,' said the priest. 'It took me by surprise.'

Ay and Horemheb looked at him a little longer, clearly unsure if the priest was telling them the truth. Eventually, they decided to leave. 'Well,' Ay told the priest, 'if you see anyone at all, you must tell us immediately.'

'Of course,' said the priest, bowing his head to show he understood.

Ay and Horemheb left the room and the priest turned around to look down at Charlie, George, Paige and

Sheena. 'I'm Wennefer,' he said. 'I am High Priest of Amun here at Karnak, and I am at your service.' He bowed a little as he spoke. 'What do you need from me?'

The friends looked at one another as they tried to work out what their next step should be. George pushed his glasses further up his nose as the priest looked down at them expectantly.

'Can you sneak us into the royal palace?' asked George.

The priest stared down at them, and then at the green eyes that looked back into his from the bag in Paige's lap. Then his face broke into a broad smile. 'But of course!' he said.

CHAPTER FIFTEEN

It was the following evening. The group had enjoyed a restful sleep and a calm day at Karnak, safe in the knowledge that Ay and Horemheb had given up their search of that particular area, and Wennefer had promised to protect them. Now, night had fallen once more and, under the cover of darkness, the priest had taken them back across the river and once more into the royal palace.

Charlie, George, Sheena and Paige followed Wennefer, their heads bowed beneath the deep hoods and cloaks the priest had given them to wear.

'A priest's head should be clean shaven,' Wennefer had told them, looking at their hair. 'As long as you do not remove the hoods, you should be fine.'

They approached a palace guard and Wennefer reminded them not to draw attention to themselves. 'Don't make eye contact with anyone,' he whispered. 'Especially you,' he said, looking directly at Paige. 'Your eyes will certainly draw attention. I have never seen eyes the colour of lapis before.'

'What's lapis?' Paige asked Charlie, who was walking beside her.

'Lapis lazuli,' replied Charlie. 'It's a semi-precious stone often used by wealthy ancient Egyptians in their tombs and in their jewellery. It's deep blue.'

'Quiet,' Wennefer warned them. 'Leave the talking to me.'

He approached the guard with confidence. 'I am here to see Pharaoh,' Wennefer said to the guard. 'Myself and my fellow priests need to speak with him urgently.'

Beside Wennefer, the four friends kept their heads bowed as low as possible and were silent.

The guard who now stood before them seemed uncertain of what to do.

'What is wrong with you?' Wennefer asked him. 'I must see Pharaoh.'

The guard bowed. 'I understand, my lord, it's just that...'

'Just that what?' said Wennefer, losing patience. 'Have you forgotten that I am the High Priest of Amun?'

'Forgive me,' said the guard. 'But Pharaoh is not well, and Ay has ordered me not to allow visitors.'

From beneath their hoods, Charlie caught Paige's eye.

'Well I am not a visitor. I am High Priest and have a right to speak with Pharaoh. Indeed, if he is unwell, it is important that I do meet with him.' Wennefer stared at the guard, whose face looked anxious. 'What is wrong with Tutankhamun?' asked the priest.

'Forgive me,' said the guard, bowing his head again. 'I am not certain. He has taken to his bed and has been there all day. All I know is that he is unable to perform his duties and is seriously ill.'

Just as the guard was delivering his news, a scream echoed around the palace.

'Ankhesenamun!' said the guard urgently, as he looked in the direction of the sound and then back to Wennefer, trying to decide what to do. In the end, he chose to run towards the scream and allow the priests to go with him. 'Something is wrong!' he shouted. 'Follow me!'

Wennefer and his little band of priests did as the guard asked and they ran behind him through rooms and corridors, towards the back of the palace.

'Who is Ankhesenamun?' asked Sheena as they ran.

'Tutankhamun's wife,' replied Wennefer. 'And his sister.'

'He married his sister?' asked George, unable to hide his surprise.

'Of course,' said the priest, trying to catch his breath as they ran. 'It is quite usual, I can assure you. Many pharaohs marry family members. Tutankhamun's father and mother were also blood relatives.'

'Ew,' Paige pulled a face. 'You'd never get me to marry one of my brothers,' she said. 'I'd rather put my head in a blender. They're all so annoying!'

They reached a door, which the guard pulled open, and they all ran into what they now realised was the Pharaoh's bedchamber. The walls were covered in huge, blue ankhs with a red and white striped pattern between them. The floor was covered in white and blue flowers, and the ceiling was decorated with blue swirls. An image of the vulture headed goddess Nekhbet, protector of the pharaohs, also looked down from the ceiling. In front of them, was the Pharaoh's golden bed, its legs shaped like those of a lion. On one side of the bed, stood Ay, his head held high as his stony face showed little emotion. Opposite him, and sat on a stool pulled up close to the bed, was Ankhesenamun. With her right hand, she grasped the hand of the Pharaoh, whilst her left hand brushed tears from her grief-stricken face. In the bed, lay Tutankhamun himself, lying on his back with his arms motionless by his sides and his eyes staring lifelessly up towards the ceiling.

As they burst into the room, the guard and the priests stared at the figure in the bed but there was no sign that he was breathing.

'He's dead!' said Ankhesenamun. 'My dear husband, and our much-loved Pharaoh, is dead!'

The guard took a step back and placed his hand across his mouth in shock. 'But he is so young!' he said in surprise.

'What is to be done?' asked Ankhesenamun through her tears. 'A pharaoh's tomb takes a lifetime to build. Tutankhamun's tomb is not yet ready for him. We have nowhere to lay his body.'

Ay looked across at Ankhesenamun, his face still showing little emotion. 'I will see to it.'

Ankhesenamun lifted her head to look straight at Ay, a look of fear now showing on her face. 'You?' she asked Ay. 'Why would *you* see to it? Surely Pharaoh's successor should be the one to prepare his tomb.'

Ay walked slowly over to Ankhesenamun and placed his hand heavily on her shoulder. 'Pharaoh has no children, no heir to rule after him. I have served him well and his trust in me has prepared me well for what I must now do.'

Ankhesenamun didn't move.

Ay moved his hand and placed it beneath her chin, lifting her head to look up at him. 'Tutankhamun is dead,' he said to her. 'For the sake of Egypt, there can be no uncertainty over who will rule next. I am ready to take on that burden and protect our beloved Egypt. And you,' he said to Ankhesenamun, lowering his voice, 'must do your duty also. You must marry his rightful successor.' Ay placed his hand back on Ankhesenamun's shoulder and squeezed it hard. 'I must go,' he said. 'There is much to do.' And with that, Ay marched past the guard, past the dead Tutankhamun without so much as a glance at his lifeless body, and past the priests who stood watching in disbelief. 'It seems you arrived too late, Wennefer,' he said, as he headed for the door. And then he was gone.

CHAPTER SIXTEEN

'Did anyone get a good look at Tutankhamun's body before the guard made us leave the room?' George asked the others.

'No,' said Charlie. 'Did anyone else?'

Paige, Sheena and George shook their heads. They hadn't been in the bed chamber for long, and now only Ankhesenamun remained beside the body of the Pharaoh, weeping behind the closed door.

Wennefer had returned to Karnak, the sudden news making it important that he return quickly to his priestly duties. The group had thanked him for his offer to go with him back to Karnak, but they knew they had other things to do.

'You are most welcome,' the priest had said to them. 'If I can be of any more help, you know where to find me.'

'We do,' agreed George. 'And you have honoured the gods by helping us as much as you have.'

Wennefer had looked pleased with George's words, and led them to a quiet room in the palace before he left. 'Priests of Amun have power,' he told them, 'and you have a right to be in the royal palace. It is unlikely anyone will come into this room but if they do, just make it clear that you are priests of Karnak. Tell them that Wennefer has asked you to stay at the palace to be of help after the tragic death of the Pharaoh, and they will leave you alone. Just remember,' he had reminded them, 'do not remove your hoods. If they see your hair they will know that you are lying about being priests.'

'Thank you,' Charlie had said. 'We won't forget.'

Wennefer had nodded and headed out of the room. 'I will send one of my assistants with food and water,' he said, as he closed the door behind him. And with that, they had found themselves once more alone in the royal palace without Wennefer to protect them.

Now they sat in a circle, looking at each other from beneath deep hoods, as they discussed what had happened. The cat was curled up happily in Sheena's lap.

'I can't believe we have just seen Tutankhamun dead!' said Charlie, excited by the whole thing. And then, remembering what they were there to do he suddenly felt deflated. 'The problem is,' he said, 'we need to find out *how* he died, and we still don't know.'

'Well, let's look at the evidence so far,' said George. 'On our way to Karnak, we said that Tutankhamun might have had an accident. Does that still seem like a good explanation for his death?'

'I know we said that the pictures of the Pharaoh hunting, riding a chariot and fighting in battle might not be real, and might just be to show him in a positive light, but we did steal his chariot - so Tutankhamun definitely had one of those!' offered Sheena. 'If he had a chariot, then it is likely that he used it and could have fallen from it. That chariot is fast! I wouldn't fancy the chances of anyone who fell off it!'

Charlie nodded enthusiastically. 'But then, when we overheard Ay and Horemheb talking at Karnak, they said the chariot was a gift from another king. Maybe Tutankhamun just kept it for show, or used it for things like processions to make himself look grand in front of the people?'

'Well he may not have fought in battle,' said Sheena. 'It sounded as though Horemheb is in charge of warfare.'

'True,' said George. 'But just because Horemheb is in charge of the army doesn't mean Tutankhamun never fought as well. Perhaps Tutankhamun only fought in some of the battles? After all, you can't expect the King to be away from Egypt all the time - and fighting wars is a full-time business.'

'So we still can't be sure whether he hunted, rode chariots or fought in battle?' asked Paige. 'That means we still don't know whether he died from having an accident when doing any of those things. It seems possible, but we can't say for sure.'

'Well we know he had a bad foot or leg when we saw him,' said Charlie, barely able to sit still because he was so excited to be trying to work out the answer to one of history's biggest questions.

'And we still don't know whether that was caused by an accident or an illness,' said Sheena.

'Or both,' added George. 'It could still be that Tutankhamun had an accident that caused a broken leg, and the break got infected and the infection killed him. If he did get an infection like that, ancient Egyptian doctors wouldn't have been able to save him.'

'OK,' said Paige, looking thoughtful. 'We still can't be sure whether he had an accident or an infection. What about illness apart from infection? Does any of the evidence tell us anything about that?'

They all became thoughtful. In Sheena's lap, the cat stood up, turned around, and then lay back down again, purring.

'What's your name, kitten?' Sheena said to it as she stroked its head. The kitten looked up at her and then put its head back down on its paw. 'She's so small,' said Sheena to the others. 'I wonder where her parents are?'

George sat up straight as Sheena spoke. 'That's it!' said George. 'That could explain things!'

'What could explain things?' asked Charlie, as they all looked at George expectantly.

'Tutankhamun's parents,' explained George. 'Didn't Wennefer say they were blood relatives?'

'Yes,' said Paige. 'He also said that Tutankhamun was married to his sister.' Paige shuddered as she spoke. 'Most days, I could punch my brothers,' she said.

'What's your point, George?' asked Sheena, leaning in with interest.

'Blood relatives having children together can lead to genetic problems for the child,' explained George. 'It can make the children weaker and more likely to have ill-nesses.'

'So you think Tutankhamun was ill because his mother and father were related?' asked Charlie.

'It's possible,' said George.

The others watched as Sheena dived into her bag and pulled out her phone. 'Here's the photo of that image we were looking at when we were hiding in Karnak,' she said. 'Given what we've learnt, I think this is a picture of Akhenaten, Tutankhamun's father, and his family. And you have to admit,' she said, holding the phone out for the others to take a closer look, 'they do all look very unusual. Maybe the wide hips and long heads were because of an illness?'

'Or maybe the artist just made them look that way,' said Paige. 'Maybe Akhenaten just wanted to send out a message about himself and his family, just like Charlie said they sometimes did when they painted a pharaoh fighting in battle or riding a chariot. Maybe Akhenaten had the artist make him look like that on purpose.'

'But what message does this send?' asked Sheena, disagreeing with Paige. 'Why would you want an artist to make you look like this when you don't?'

Paige shook her head, 'I'm not sure. I just think it's something to keep in mind.'

'Did anyone notice if Tutankhamun had wider hips or an unusual shaped head, like this picture suggests?' asked Charlie.

The others shook their heads.

'He was wearing a long tunic and a headdress when we saw him in the throne room,' George reminded them, 'so we couldn't tell. And we couldn't get a close enough look when his body was lying in his bed.'

'So we can't be sure of that either,' said Charlie, feeling frustrated.

'Mosquitos!' Paige shouted, breaking the silence. 'Maybe the mosquitos killed him!'

George's face lit up. 'Of course, Paige! Perhaps it's the mosquitos!'

'Why would mosquitos want to kill the Pharaoh?' asked Sheena. 'I mean, I can think of lots of reasons why someone might want to kill a king but I can't think why mosquitos would be bothered.'

Paige stared at Sheena. 'Are you serious?' she asked, her frown evidence that she was trying to decide whether Sheena was making a joke.

'What?' asked Sheena in return. 'You and George think the mosquitos killed him. I'm just waiting to hear why.'

Paige sighed and turned back to George. 'We noticed mosquitos at Karnak,' she said.

'But we used insect repellent,' added George, his enthusiasm matching Paige's.

'Something the ancient Egyptians don't have,' said Paige.

'Exactly!' said George. 'And what illness do mosquitos cause?' he asked.

Charlie and Sheena looked at George and Paige but said nothing. Sheena shrugged.

'Malaria!' said Paige. 'They cause Malaria!'

'And could that kill him?' asked Charlie.

'It could, yes,' George answered him. 'It would cause a dangerous fever and lots of other symptoms, like a headache and feeling sick - all things which would cause a person to take to their bed.' He leant back and patted Paige on the arm, pleased with the idea. 'It can also live in a person's system for a long time. And it can keep making them ill over and over again, assuming it hasn't killed them, of course!'

'Would it explain the bad leg?' asked Charlie.

George's face fell a little as Charlie asked the question. 'No, I don't think so.'

'So perhaps Tutankhamun had an accident or illness that caused his bad leg, and also had Malaria,' Sheena suggested. 'Maybe he didn't die from just one thing.'

'This is getting complicated,' said George. 'I thought it would be more straight forward than this.' George took off his glasses and rubbed his eyes.

'There is the other option we mentioned,' said Charlie, looking them all in the eye.

'You mean,' asked Sheena in a whisper, 'murder?'

'That's exactly what I mean,' said Charlie, feeling more confident about his theory after all they had seen and heard. 'You heard Ay and Horemheb at Karnak. They were obviously angry that they do all the work and get none of the credit. Ay even said that one of them should rule after Tutankhamun - and they are both older than the Pharaoh. Why would they expect to live longer than him and be able to rule Egypt when he dies?'

'And they did try to capture us,' added Sheena, picking up the cat and hugging her tight. 'What do you think they would do to us if they caught us?' she asked the others, and their faces looked frightened at the thought.

'The question,' said Paige, 'is why they would want to kill Tutankhamun? I understand why they want to capture us, we found our way into the royal palace and then stole the Pharaoh's chariot, but why would anyone want to kill Tutankhamun?'

'Like they said at Karnak,' Sheena offered, 'they think they do all the work and deserve to be recognised for it.'

'Or because of Tutankhamun's father,' suggested Charlie. 'From everything we've learnt, it seems clear that Akhenaten angered people by refusing to worship Amun, and insisting there was only one god - the Aten. He dishonoured the gods. He also upset the priests of Amun who lost all their power and wealth because of what he did. What wealthy and powerful priest wouldn't want to see Amun back in his rightful place?'

'That may explain why a priest would want to kill Akhenaten,' said George. 'But Tutankhamun was trying to restore the buildings that Akhenaten knocked down, and so was honouring the gods again. He even changed his name from Tutankhaten to Tutankhamun - you heard Ay say so! It looks like Tutankhamun was trying to put Egypt back together, so why kill him for it?'

'Maybe some people still don't trust him because of what his father did?' suggested Paige. 'Maybe someone wanted to be sure the whole family was wiped out and would never again make Egypt worship the Aten.'

'Or maybe,' said Charlie, 'some people just want power for themselves - and will do anything to get it.'

Sheena turned to Charlie. 'So you think Ay and Horemheb just want the throne for themselves?'

'I'm not sure of their reasons,' answered Charlie. 'But yes, I think they want more power. And of the two, my money is on Ay. Did you hear what he said to Ankhesenamun in the Pharaoh's bed chamber? He practically told everyone in the room that he was the next pharaoh and that Ankhesenamun would now have to marry him, just to prove it. And he said all that when Tutankhamun had only just taken his final breath.'

The others nodded. They too had heard what Ay had said. 'I didn't see Horemheb in the bed chamber,' said Sheena. 'Where do you think he is?'

'I overheard the guards earlier,' said George. 'Apparently, he had to leave Egypt again to lead the army in another battle. He doesn't know the Pharaoh is dead.'

'Then, when Ay said to Horemheb that one of the two of them should rule next, he really meant himself,' said Charlie. 'He didn't leave much chance for Horemheb to become the next ruler, did he? He took the opportunity of the Pharaoh's death and Horemheb's absence to take the throne for himself.' Charlie folded his arms. 'I don't like him,' he continued, 'and I definitely do not trust him.'

As Charlie finished speaking there was a noise on the other side of the door. They all turned in the direction of the noise and watched as the door opened just a fraction and then stopped. Then they heard voices.

'Are you well, my lady?' a woman asked.

'Yes, thank you,' another woman replied but her voice sounded as though she had been crying.

The first voice dropped to little more than a whisper. 'Ankhesenamun, are you sure?' The voice dropped lower still, 'I am afraid for you.'

Ankhesenamun whispered back, so quiet they could barely hear. 'I am afraid too. But I am hopeful.'

The two voices stopped and there was complete silence. At that moment, the cat curled up in Sheena's lap leapt up and made her way to the door. Sheena tried to stop her but it was too late. The kitten scurried across the room and through the crack in the door, much to the delight of the women outside.

'Mau Mau,' they heard Ankhesenamun's voice say. 'Where have you been, little one? I have been looking for you.' The cat meowed in reply. 'You see,' said Ankhesenamun to the other woman. 'There is reason to be hopeful. Mau Mau was missing but she has come back to me - and now I am not alone.'

'I am glad,' said the second woman. 'But what is the reason for this hope? What are you going to do?'

Ankhesenamun began whispering again. 'I have written to a neighbouring king,' she told the other woman. 'I have asked him to send me his son for a husband.'

'You have asked for a foreigner to become Pharaoh of Egypt?' asked the second woman, clearly shocked. 'But that is not done, Ankhesenamun.'

Ankhesenamun answered in a whisper so quiet that Charlie, George, Paige and Sheena could barely hear it. Charlie pulled his hood away from his ear, and still only just caught Ankhesenamun's words.

'I am the widow of a pharaoh, and I will not marry Ay,' she said with a mixture of fear and determination in her voice. 'I will not marry a servant.'

CHAPTER SEVENTEEN

'It's time to get up,' whispered Paige to the rest of them as they lay dozing on the cold floor. 'It's getting light.'

'That was so uncomfortable,' said George, sounding happy that the night was over. 'I'm sick of sleeping on this cold, hard floor. We've been here for three weeks now!'

'I know what you mean,' said Charlie, as he slowly sat up. 'I try to lie on my cloak as much as I can, but it doesn't help.'

On the other side of the room, Sheena also sat up slowly but she didn't speak.

'Are you ok, Sheena?' Charlie asked her as she wiped a tear from beneath her eye.

'I'm fine,' sniffed Sheena. 'I still miss the kitten - Mau Mau.' She looked down at the floor, 'I love cats but we aren't allowed to have pets at home.' Two more big tears trickled down her cheeks. 'I want to go home. I didn't think we'd be away so long. And we still don't know for sure how Tutankhamun died, even after spending all this time at the palace.'

'Don't worry, Sheena,' said Charlie, as he put his arm around her and the others came to stand close. 'Remember that time isn't passing in the same way at home. When we get back to Crankhall Lane, it will still be dawn at the abbey on the day we left to come to Egypt. No one will even know we left. At least, that's what the book said. And we have to believe in the book.'

'And remember that Ankhesenamun isn't alone now she has her cat back,' said Paige. 'She sounded really happy to have found Mau Mau.'

Sheena nodded. 'That's true.'

'It's a strange name, Mau Mau,' said Paige. 'What do you think it means?'

'Mau means 'cat' in ancient Egyptian,' Charlie told them. 'I know because my auntie Mariam has a cat in Cairo, and she named it Mau.'

'It sounds a bit like meow, doesn't it?' George said, thoughtfully. He sighed. 'We've been lucky again. We made it through another night without anyone trying to get into the room.'

'They couldn't have got in anyway,' Charlie reminded him. 'We lock the door from the inside.'

'I know,' replied George. 'But if someone had tried to get in and realised the door was locked from the inside, they'd have thought it was strange - and then they might have found out we were here.'

'I thought it was ok for priests to be in the royal palace,' said Paige.

'That's what Wennefer told us, yes,' George agreed. 'But I doubt if it's normal for a group of priests to be sleeping on the floor of one of the palace rooms.'

'Well, we do the right thing and one of us is always awake and on guard,' said Paige. 'At least we'd have some warning if anyone were about to find us.' She looked around the room and then pointed to the back wall. 'If it happened, we could go out of that window.' She sighed. 'Maybe it's time we headed back to the portal. I'm not sure we can find out much more here.'

George nodded. 'I think you might be right.'

Charlie stood up and went to look through the window. He had to stand on tiptoes to see out but he could just see the large courtyard outside. It stood in shadows because the sky was still quite dark and the rising sun had only just begun to streak its flashes of red and orange across the horizon. Nevertheless, people were still beginning their work for the day.

'The people are outside working,' said Charlie to the others. 'Why do you think they start so early? Do you think it's usual, or do you think it's because the Pharaoh has died and there's so much to do?'

George shrugged. 'Maybe they always start early because of the heat,' he said as he walked over to join Charlie. George was tall enough to see right out but he stood to the side, peeping out instead. 'Everyone looks too busy to notice me,' he said 'but you can never be too careful.'

'What's happening out there?' asked Paige as she and Sheena joined the others to look.

They watched as more and more people arrived in the courtyard, all of them gathering countless different items and arranging them in neat piles. There were groups of chariots, piles of hunting equipment, and weapons for fighting in battle. They could see furniture and jewellery, jars of make-up and perfumes, games and clothes, food and wine, musical instruments, lamps and statues of all sizes, and a pile of walking sticks.

'That is a lot of stuff!' said Charlie, staring out the window.

'Put your hood up, Charlie!' Paige exclaimed. 'Remember what Wennefer told us - if they see your hair they'll know you're not a priest!'

'Sorry, I forgot,' Charlie replied, feeling silly, and he pulled the hood quickly over his head.

As the four of them stood gazing in wonder at the growing piles of items outside, there was a gentle knock at the door. They all turned away from the window and stared, wide eyed, in the direction of the noise. None of them spoke. Then the knock came again.

Next they heard a quiet voice. 'Are you still in there?'

'That's Wennefer,' said Charlie in relief as he walked across the room and unlocked the door.

Wennefer stepped quickly inside and closed the door behind him. 'I wasn't sure you would all still be here,' he said to them. 'But I'm glad to find that you haven't left. I had a dream last night that you needed my help, so I came back to check on you. Is all well?'

'Yes, thank you,' said Charlie.

Wennefer smiled broadly. 'That is good news,' he said. 'I trust my junior priests have kept bringing you supplies, as I instructed?'

'They have, yes,' said George. 'We are grateful to you, and to them.' George turned his attention back to the window.

'We were just looking at everything going on in the courtyard,' Charlie told the priest. 'We can't believe just how much stuff there is out there!'

Wennefer moved over to the window and glanced through. 'That is nothing!' he said, waving his hand to emphasise his point. 'That is just a small part of everything that the Pharaoh will need in the afterlife.'

'You mean, that is all for Tutankhamun?' asked Sheena.

Wennefer nodded his head. 'Of course,' he said. 'In life he has been used to being surrounded by all of these things, why should he not have them in the next life also? He is Pharaoh, after all.'

'But what will he do with them all?' asked Paige.

'The same as he did with them here,' Wennefer told her. 'He is going to the afterlife - he will need plenty to keep him busy!'

'So you really do believe there's a life after death?' asked Paige.

'Of course there is a life afterwards,' said Wennefer. 'You of all people should know! The gods have sent you after all!' Wennefer looked at them and then took a sharp breath. 'Perhaps the gods sent you here to test me? Is that why you are here? To test my respect for the gods and all they have taught me?' He looked worried.

'We're not testing you, Wennefer,' said Paige, looking uncomfortable at her mistake. 'I just wondered what you thought.'

'And now you know,' said Wennefer, looking nervous. 'A person has so much to offer the world. Each one of us has so many gifts and talents, and so many people that love us and that we love in return. We are so much more than just our bodies. Why would death be the end of us? Of course there is more after! That is,' he continued 'so long as the person is able to pass the Weighing of the Heart Ceremony.'

'Where the dead person's heart is weighed against a feather,' said Charlie.

'Exactly!' Wennefer replied wagging his finger. 'But not just any feather - the feather of Maat, the goddess of truth and justice! We must all do our best to live a good life,' he advised them 'so that when our hearts are eventually placed on the scales against Maat's feather, the scales will balance. Then the gods will reward us with a place in the afterlife.'

'And you think Tutankhamun will pass the test?' asked Paige.

'Certainly,' said Wennefer. 'He is Pharaoh. He is already protected by the gods.'

'And will he be able to eat and drink all that food and wine too?' asked Sheena, looking back through the window. The piles of items kept growing and growing. 'There's a lot there.'

'Eternity is a long time!' answered Wennefer. 'And certainly he will be able to eat and drink the food and wine that is buried with him in his tomb. He'll be able to eat and drink it just as soon as Ay has performed the Opening of the Mouth Ceremony on Tutankhamun's body. That is the point of the Opening of the Mouth Ritual - to make sure the dead person will be able to eat and drink and breathe again.'

Paige looked at the priest. 'And you said Ay will perform this ritual?'

'Yes,' said Wennefer. 'It is custom for the next king to perform the Opening of the Mouth Ritual for the dead pharaoh.

'So Ay is definitely going to rule next,' Charlie whispered to Sheena, who nodded.

'And all of those things and more besides will fit in the tomb?' asked George, still peering out of the window with apparent interest.

'They will fit,' said Wennefer, 'although it may be a tight squeeze. Tutankhamun's tomb should have been bigger than the one he will receive, but because no one expected him to die so young, work on his own, bigger, tomb has not even begun. Fortunately, Ay has made sure Tutankhamun will be buried in a good tomb. He is preparing it as we speak.'

Charlie looked at Sheena again as Wennefer mentioned Ay's name for a second time.

'And where is the tomb?' asked George.

'In the usual place,' replied Wennefer. 'Tutankhamun will be buried not far from here. He will be laid to rest in the same place as all the other pharaohs of recent years.'

'The Valley of the Kings,' Charlie whispered to Sheena. 'The famous necropolis.'

'What's a necropolis?' Sheena asked.

'It means 'city of the dead' in Greek,' George told her.

'Lovely,' said Sheena. 'I think I'll give it a miss.'

'Where's Tutankhamun now, Wennefer?' asked Charlie.

'He is in the embalming hall,' replied the priest. 'They have started the mummification process. It usually takes around seventy days from start to finish, so they have a long way to go. They have removed the organs though. And...' Wennefer stopped, apparently unsure whether to say what was on his mind.

'And, what?' asked Paige.

Wennefer looked at each of them and then behind him, making sure the door was fully closed. He lowered his voice as he spoke. 'A junior priest I know is helping to mummify Tutankhamun's body,' he said. 'And there is something strange.'

'What do you mean, strange?' asked Charlie, as they all huddled in closer to hear Wennefer.

'They removed his heart,' whispered the priest. 'And they cut some of his ribs.'

'Would they need to cut the ribs to be able to remove the heart?' asked George.

'It's possible,' said Wennefer.

'But why did they remove his heart in the first place?' asked Charlie, knowing how unusual this was.

Wennefer shook his head, 'I don't know. I'm sure they have their reasons but I don't know what they are.'

'But Pharaoh will need his heart to get into the afterlife,' said Charlie.

'That's true,' Wennefer replied, nodding his head. 'This is indeed an unusual case but if, for some reason unknown to me, they have had to remove the heart from the body, they will surely place it in a jar and bury it with the Pharaoh. That way, he will still have his heart with him.' He looked behind him again. 'But that is not all,' he continued.

The others said nothing but leant in further.

Wennefer took a deep breath. 'There was a hole in Pharaoh's skull.'

'A hole?' said Charlie.

'Yes,' replied Wennefer. 'I don't know how it got there. There could be many explanations. It could even have been done accidentally as they mummified him, perhaps as they removed the brain. It's just...unusual.'

'Where in his skull is the hole?' asked George.

'At the back of the head,' said Wennefer.

'But they remove the brain through the nose,' said Charlie.

Wennefer nodded in agreement. 'Indeed,' he replied.

They all stared at him and then at each other, unsure what to think.

'Thank you for telling us, Wennefer. This information is very useful,' said George. 'It seems we did need your help after all.'

'I am glad to be of service to the gods and those they send to me,' replied Wennefer. 'Is there anything more I can do for you?'

'We need to leave this room and the palace without being seen,' said George. 'I think we need to make it to the palace gardens, by the lake.' He looked at the others and they nodded. It was time to go, and the lake was a good place to hide and decide what to do next. 'Can you walk with us that far?'

'It will be my pleasure,' said the priest, bowing. 'I am glad to have helped you.'

'You have been a great help,' said George. 'The gods will be pleased with all you have done.'

Wennefer smiled again and looked proud of himself. 'Follow me,' he said. 'And make sure you all have a hood upon your heads.'

They all did as they were asked and Charlie, followed by George, Sheena and Paige, walked behind the priest as he pulled open the door to the little room and stepped out into the space beyond.

As they began to make their way through the palace, footsteps came towards them and the four friends lowered their heads to avoid being seen.

'Hello, Wennefer,' a familiar voice greeted the priest.

'Hello, General,' Wennefer replied. 'It is good to see you back safe from the battlefield.'

From beneath their hoods, they all instantly recognised the voice of Horemheb, who simply grunted in response. 'I am only here for a short time. I have come to find Ay.'

'And you have found me,' said another familiar and frightening voice. And Horemheb walked off towards Ay, apparently disinterested in Wennefer and the other four priests who walked with him.

'Can we stop for a moment,' asked Paige as they reached a group of large columns. 'I'm sorry. It's just with sleeping on the hard floor, I've now got cramp in my leg.'

'Of course,' said Wennefer, concerned. 'Here, sit down.'

Paige sat on the nearby stone bench that stood against a wall and behind several columns that were painted red, white and blue and stretched from floor to ceiling. From here, they could not be seen by others in the room. Ay and Horemheb would think they had left.

The others shot Paige a knowing look and were grateful for her quick thinking. Past the columns, standing some distance away and talking in voices so quiet no one could hear, were Ay and Horemheb. The group couldn't tell what the pair were saying, but their sinister looks and bowed heads told them they were up to something.

Just then, another set of footsteps entered the room through a doorway at the far end. 'Ah, Ankhesenamun,' Ay greeted her. 'General Horemheb is back from battle until Tutankhamun has been buried. Isn't that good news?'

Ankhesenamun looked surprised, as though she hadn't expected the men to be there. 'Of course,' she said. 'It is always good to know Egypt's greatest general is home safely.'

Ay didn't take his gaze from Ankhesenamun. 'I have put everything in place for Tutankhamun's funeral,' he said to her, looking interested in her response. 'I have arranged a tomb which will be finished in time, and I have asked that the paintings inside the tomb show me performing the Opening of the Mouth Ceremony for Tutankhamun. The death mask will also be ready for him.'

Ankhesenamun stared silently back at Ay before she responded. 'Thank you,' she said, bowing her head a little. 'I am sure my husband would be grateful for all you are doing for him.' And with that, Ankhesenamun began to walk away.

'One more thing,' Ay shouted after her. 'I have heard that you recently wrote to a neighbouring king.'

Ankhesenamun stopped dead but she didn't turn around.

'When the King received your letter, it seems he sent his son to marry you.' Ay glared at Ankhesenamun's back but she didn't move an inch. 'It's a dangerous journey, crossing all that land to get to Thebes,' Ay continued. 'Anyone making that journey would have to travel a long way and pass through areas that are at war, where battles are being fought. That would be a dangerous journey indeed. Anything could happen to someone trying to make it.'

Ankhesenamun finally turned around to look at Ay, her face filled with fear and anger.

Ay had a cruel smile on his face. 'It is I who will be accompanying you to Tutankhamun's funeral, Ankhesenamun. And it is I who will be the next to sit on the throne of Egypt,' he continued, his eyes never leaving Ankhesenamun's and the smile never leaving his face. 'I am sorry to be the bearer of more bad news, Ankhesenamun,' he said, before pausing, as if he were enjoying the moment. 'But the husband you asked for, is dead.'

CHAPTER EIGHTEEN

Ankhesenamun left the room. Ay and Horemheb watched as she practically ran back through the far doorway, and then they began talking to one another in hushed tones.

'So Ankhesenamun asked a neighbouring king to send her a husband?' said Wennefer to the others quietly, apparently shocked at the thought. 'That is most unusual. No queen of Egypt would marry a foreign prince. It is unheard of!'

'Then she must have found herself in very difficult circumstances,' answered George thoughtfully.

Charlie nodded in agreement. It seemed they all knew far more than Wennefer.

Suddenly the conversation between Ay and Horemheb became a little louder, their voices showing disagreement.

'I had to act,' Ay whispered loudly. 'You were not here, Horemheb.'

'How convenient,' spat Horemheb. 'You were supposed to wait. We agreed we would carry out the plan together.'

Ay glared back at Horemheb before softening his voice and placing his hands on Horemheb's shoulders. 'Our plan has worked perfectly, Horemheb. One of us had to rule first and, as Vizier, it makes sense that it should be me. No one will suspect anything. Tutankhamun is dead, and you have removed the only threat to our plan - the foreign husband Ankhesenamun requested.' Ay dropped his hands. 'Did you do it yourself?'

'Of course,' replied Horemheb, his voice still sounding angry. 'He was dead almost as soon as he had set out for Egypt.'

Ay lowered his voice. 'How did you do it? I've found that a sudden and unexpected blow to the back of the head is highly effective!'

Horemheb grunted. 'But apparently not instant,' he said. 'Lucky for us, Tutankhamun didn't recover.' His eyes were filled with fire as he answered Ay's question. 'I dealt with it like a soldier - with a spear as I looked my enemy in the eye.' He stared at Ay, never lowering his gaze. 'I was not going to allow a foreign prince anywhere near my beloved Egypt. I have not won countless victories in battle just to watch Egypt fall into the wrong hands.'

'Egypt will stay safe in your capable hands, General,' said Ay, smiling. 'And when I take the throne, I shall name you as my successor. Then, when the time comes, Egypt will be safe under your rule as its king.'

Horemheb looked back at Ay and then bowed his head, apparently resigning himself to his situation. 'Yes, Pharaoh.'

Charlie looked wide eyed at his companions as he realised they had just received proof that he had been right all along - Ay had killed Tutankhamun. And it seems he had done it with a blow to the head - and from behind, when he least expected it. 'Coward,' whispered Charlie angrily.

'Come,' said Wennefer, looking fearful because of all they had just heard. 'We should leave, and quickly. We can get to the gardens that way.' He gestured with his hand to show them the direction, and they all started to follow him. In that instant, Ay looked across to the doorway and saw the silent movement behind the columns.

'Who's there?' shouted Ay, heading over to the columns with Horemheb at his side.

'Quickly,' said Wennefer. 'Keep moving.'

They did as Wennefer asked and in his haste, Charlie didn't notice his hood slide from his head.

'Stop!' Horemheb shouted behind them. 'You are not a priest!'

They all stopped dead, and Charlie gasped as he realised that Ay and Horemheb had finally found them.

'Wennefer, why do you help him to pretend in this way?' Ay continued to walk slowly towards them, squinting his eyes to get a better look at the faces of the people beneath the hoods. Then a look of recognition crossed his face. 'That's them, Horemheb!' shouted Ay. 'These are the ones we have been looking for - the ones who stole from this palace!' As Ay finished speaking, he broke into a run and Horemheb began to follow him.

'Quick,' said Wennefer. 'Follow me! And run!'

'Not again!' said Sheena as they found themselves running away, once again, from Ay and Horemheb.

'Stop talking Sheena!' yelled George. 'Save your breath for running!'

'Running is all we've done!' Sheena shouted back. 'Miss Barber would be proud of us.'

'She'd be surprised,' added Paige. 'She can never get us to do any running in P.E. class.'

'You won't get away this time!' yelled Ay from close behind them.

'Quick!' said Wennefer. 'You must run faster!'

They did as they were asked, and finally they found themselves running once more out of the main palace entrance and into the courtyard where they had found the chariot.

Just as they began to run across it, Paige tripped and went tumbling across the stones. 'Ow!' she shouted, as she fell.

Sheena saw Paige first. 'Stop!' she shouted to the others. 'Paige has fallen!'

The others slowed and turned around just as they saw Ay appear right behind Paige, with Horemheb close on his heels.

'Get up, Paige!' shouted Charlie as they began to run back towards her to help. 'They're right behind you!'

Paige made an effort to scramble to her feet, and almost made it before Ay threw himself forward and grabbed hold of her leg.

'Get off me!' yelled Paige, as she pulled up her other leg and kicked Ay square in the stomach. The kick forced him to let go of Paige's leg and sent him reeling backwards in surprise. Paige took her moment and got to her feet. The others watched as she started to run again but found that something else was holding her back. Behind her, Horemheb had now caught up with Ay and had grabbed firmly onto the edge of her cloak, making it impossible for her to move forward. Shock crossed her face and then, in a moment of quick thinking, she opened the cloak's fastening at her neck and sprinted away, leaving Horemheb standing behind her and gripping the empty cloak in his fist.

'Keep going!' she shouted to the others. 'Just run!'

'You go that way,' Wennefer said to them, when they had put a little more ground between them and Ay and Horemheb. 'The lake is over there. Get past those trees there and they'll lose sight of you. I'll run that way,' he said, pointing in the opposite direction from the lake.

'Hopefully, they'll see me and follow. Then you can find a place to hide.'

'But what about you?' asked Charlie.

'I'll be fine,' said Wennefer. 'I am High Priest of Amun - I'll think of something to tell them. And anyway,' he said, running short of breath, 'you said the gods will shower blessings down on me for helping you.'

'Thank you, friend,' said Charlie.

Wennefer smiled broadly in return. 'Go!' he said to them. And then he was gone, and they were a group of four again.

'In here!' said George, and they all followed him into a clump of trees.

'It looks like we're back in the plants again,' commented Sheena.

'Shhh,' said Charlie. 'They're right there.'

They all fell silent and watched from amongst the bushes as Wennefer's plan worked.

'Over there!' shouted Horemheb as he caught sight of Wennefer.

'They won't get away this time!' shouted Ay.

'Wanna bet?' whispered Paige. And then Wennefer, Ay and Horemheb were gone, and they all breathed a sigh of relief.

'What now?' asked Sheena.

'Well, we know how Tutankhamun died,' said Charlie. 'We've done what we needed to do.'

'Yes,' agreed George. 'Ay killed him. And Horemheb was in on the whole thing!'

'Do you think that means Tutankhamun will be able to rest in peace now?'

Charlie nodded. 'I think so, yes. At least, that's what the book said.'

'Doesn't that mean it's time to go home, then?' asked Paige.

'And fast,' said Sheena. 'Before they find us and decide that it's a good idea to treat us in the same way they treated Tutankhamun. I don't want to die here.'

'Well we can't go back through the portal until we have the right incantation,' Charlie reminded them as he laid his bag on the ground and pulled out the book. He opened it up as the others looked at him expectantly.

'Well?' asked George.

Charlie looked through the book, and saw their time in ancient Egypt had been recorded. He turned over the pages, feeling hopeful, but when he got to the last page he looked up at his three friends and shook his head. 'There's nothing,' he said, his voice filled with worry. 'There's no incantation to get us home.'

The others stared back at him.

'So what do we do?' asked Paige.

They all looked at one another for an answer.

'We could sit and have something to eat,' suggested Sheena. 'I'm starving.'

George looked at her with one eyebrow raised.

'I haven't eaten in ages,' Sheena responded.

'Surely you haven't got any of those sandwiches still in your bag? They won't be safe to eat now,' said George.

Sheena shrugged. 'I've got other things,' she said. 'I've got some dates, for a start.'

'So where do we sit and, *eat*?' asked George, emphasising the word eat as he gave Sheena an exasperated look. 'We need somewhere we can hide whilst we figure out what to do.'

'I think we should find somewhere to hide next to the portal,' said Charlie.

The others agreed. 'It makes sense,' said George. 'And that way, we'll be ready if the incantation appears.'

'Let's go then,' said Charlie.

*****

Night had fallen and after the little group had spent hours talking, George, Sheena and Paige had finally fallen into an exhausted sleep. Charlie sat awake, keeping guard and looking out at the portal through the trees. Quietly, so as not to wake the others, he unzipped his bag and pulled out the book for the second time that day, hoping this time to find the incantation that would take them home.

In the darkness, he switched on his phone and looked at the book by its light. The phone's battery, he saw, was running low. He stared at the screen, hoping more than believing that he might see sign of a service and signal. If he wasn't going to make it home, he'd have given anything to speak to his mom and grandad one last time. He felt a lump form in his throat as he thought about them.

He swallowed and shook his head. 'Of course you can't make a call, Charlie,' he said to himself. 'You're in ancient Egypt. It will be thousands of years before the telephone is invented, let alone mobile phones.' He took a deep breath and turned his attention back to the book, knowing it was their only hope. He hurriedly turned to the end of the story so far to see if anything new had appeared. With a sharp intake of breath, he saw that it had - but it was not what he had expected. Nor was it what he wanted to read.

Well done, brave adventurer, Charlie read, holding his phone as close as possible to the page. *You have solved one of history's greatest unanswered questions. You now know what happened to the one they call the boy king.*

'It wasn't really me who solved it,' Charlie thought to himself. 'We all did it together, and we finally found out what had happened because we overheard Ay. I didn't really do anything.' He suddenly felt small.

Now, said the book, *it is time to finish this.* Charlie looked over at his friends. All three of them were still fast asleep beneath the trees. *Justice must be done*, said the book. *And it is you, Charlie Swain, who must see it done.*

'Me?' whispered Charlie under his breath. 'What can *I* do?'

It is time, Charlie, he read. And then, beneath that short sentence, was an incantation.

'Finally,' Charlie thought, breathing a sigh of relief. But the relief was soon replaced by panic as he read through the incantation.

And now I seek to end my quest, until it's done, I shall not rest.
In the desert, there it stands, the famous creature of the sands,
guarding all that has ever been, and all the world has ever seen.
Beneath its paws I now must go, to speak with those who live below.
For the sun to rise I cannot wait, take me now to that secret place.

'The famous creature of the sands,' Charlie read again, trying to work out what the incantation meant. 'A creature with paws,' he said to himself. 'A creature with paws that stands in the desert.'

Charlie heard one of his friends stir in their sleep and he looked over at them, but no one woke. He looked back at the incantation and realisation slowly dawned.

'A famous creature, with paws, that stands in the desert,' he said to himself. 'The Sphinx!' he whispered. 'It's talking about the Sphinx!'

Go alone. And go now.

Charlie saw the words and was afraid. He thought again about his mom and grandad back home.

You must see it through to the end.

Charlie felt a lump in his throat as he looked over at his sleeping friends. 'I can't go alone,' he thought. 'I need my friends. Whatever I have to do, I can't do it alone.'

Then, before his very eyes, a final sentence appeared. It was one Charlie had already read at the beginning of their adventure but the book repeated it anyway.

A hero is nothing if he does not believe.

CHAPTER NINETEEN

Paige jumped awake, sure she had heard a noise, and looked around her. It was dark, so dark in fact that the only light came from the moon and stars way up above, their gentle, silver glow only just making it through the leafy canopy of their hiding place. Nearby, George and Sheena still lay sleeping.

'Where's Charlie?' Paige said to herself, feeling panic rise. 'George, Sheena,' she whispered urgently, shaking each of them awake. 'I can't see Charlie.'

'What?' Sheena was awake instantly.

'I'm sure he's here,' said George calmly, retrieving his glasses and placing them onto his nose.

'He's not!' whispered Paige, standing up and moving over to the spot where Charlie had been sitting. 'He's gone! Look! Even his bag is missing!'

George and Sheena themselves stood up and moved over to join Paige.

'I think you're right, Paige,' said George, now looking worried.

'I told you,' said Paige, impatiently.

Sheena looked like she was about to be sick. 'You don't think Ay has him, do you?'

'I don't know,' replied Paige, herself feeling like she might throw up. 'I hope not.'

'That doesn't make any sense,' said George. 'Surely if Ay had found us, he'd have taken all of us, not just Charlie. At the very least, I think Charlie would've struggled and we'd have heard something.'

'Where is he then?' Paige demanded.

George shook his head. 'I don't know.'

The three friends looked around them, searching for a clue that might explain what had happened to Charlie.

Paige spotted something on the floor and went over to pick it up, her eyes squinting to see in the dark. 'What's this?'

The others followed her to see what she had found.

'It's a notepad,' said Paige, holding it up for the others to see. 'And the top page has been ripped out of it.'

'Let me see,' said George, holding out his hand.

Paige handed him the notepad.

'Pass me a light,' said George, and Sheena switched on her phone and handed it to George, who shone the light onto the notepad. 'There's something on the page,' said George. 'Look,' he said, pointing. 'Can you see it?'

Paige and Sheena looked down at the paper and then back at George. Both girls nodded.

'Does anyone have a pencil?' asked George.

'Here,' said Paige, as she passed him a pen.

'No,' said George. 'A pencil. It has to be a pencil.'

'I've got one,' said Sheena, going over to her bag. 'Here.'

George took the offered pencil. 'Can you hold the phone light over the paper?' he asked Paige, handing her the phone.

Paige did as she was asked and she and Sheena watched as George rubbed the pencil across the top sheet of paper on the notepad.

'What are you...?' Paige stopped as she realised she could answer her own question.

'You're so clever, George,' said Sheena.

Paige had to agree. 'There's writing on it!' she said, excitedly.

'Well, technically, there was writing on the page above this one,' said George, explaining what was happening. 'What we are seeing are the marks made by the pen or pencil on the page above, the one that has been removed.'

'Well, what does it say?' demanded Paige.

George fell quiet and studied the page. 'It's an incantation,' he said, looking up at the others.

'What kind of incantation?' asked Paige.

'Is it the one that will get us home?' asked Sheena, her voice sounding hopeful.

'I'm afraid not,' answered George, looking worried. 'But I think I know how to find Charlie.'

Paige saw Sheena's eyes grow as wide as her own. 'How?' asked Paige. 'Where is he?'

'Put it this way,' said George seriously. 'He's not with Ay.'

CHAPTER TWENTY

The huge room stretched out before Charlie as far as he could see. To either side of him, golden shelves, filled with books´the same colour as the book in Charlie's bag, stretched out into the distance. Along the centre of the room were rows of tables, some piled high with golden coloured scrolls, all tied around their centre with a deep, blue ribbon. The tables themselves gleamed a dull gold in the light cast by the torches that hung high above, up where the walls met the ceiling. Charlie's eyes followed the line of the room beyond the flames of the torches and saw a huge, vaulted ceiling arched above him, its surface painted in a dark, inky blue. The blue paint was filled with silver stars and in amongst them, a woman arched her star-sprinkled body across the night sky, her hands and feet reaching down towards the ground, her eyes looking down upon all who walked below.

'Nut,' whispered Charlie under his breath. 'Protector of the dead.'

'Exactly.'

Charlie snapped his eyes away from the ceiling and looked in the direction of the voice. He felt his shoulders and throat tense as he saw who it was that spoke. 'It's you,' he whispered, barely able to speak.

The figure nodded. 'Welcome Charlie, it is good to see you.'

In front of Charlie stood a familiar figure. His dark eyes, lined in black eyeliner, gazed at Charlie without blinking, and his bald head shone in the firelight cast by the torches' orange glow. From one ear hung a familiar looking earring. Its gold loop and cross swung from his earlobe.

Charlie couldn't believe what was happening. 'It's you! You're the man from the shop, from the bookshop on Crankhall Lane!'

The man smiled gently and gave a slight bow of his head. 'I am Japhet,' he said.

'Japhet.' Charlie repeated the name slowly. Its sound was as strange as the man's attire. A dark blue hood rested on his shoulders, and the matching robe, edged in gold, fell gracefully to his feet.

'I wasn't sure you would come through the portal alone,' he said. 'You have done well, Charlie.'

'What's going on?' asked Charlie, unsure whether the man before him was to be trusted. 'Where am I?'

'You're in the Hall of Records,' he said, matter of factly.

Charlie glanced at the books and scrolls that filled the room. 'What kind of records?' he asked suspiciously.

The man's face still carried a gentle smile. 'Records of everything,' he said, raising his eyebrows. 'Around you, Charlie,' he gestured with his hand towards the endless shelves that bordered the room, 'are records of all that has ever happened in the history of humanity.'

Charlie's frown showed his confusion.

'Every book here,' said Japhet, 'represents every life that has ever been, every life that is, and every life that will ever be. Each book is a record of everything a person ever did, of every piece of advice they ever took or ignored, of every failure, every mistake, every success, of every choice they ever made. Each one of these is called a Book of Life.'

Engrossed in what was being said and in everything around him, Charlie didn't respond.

'That is why we also sometimes call this place the Hall of Life.' Japhet fell silent, apparently waiting for Charlie to speak.

Charlie placed a hand to his face in a mixture of confusion and disbelief. 'If it's the Hall of Life, why is the goddess Nut on the ceiling? If half of these books are about people who have died, or people who haven't even been born yet, why call it the Hall of Life?'

For the first time, the man laughed. It was a loud laugh that echoed all around them. 'Charlie,' said Japhet, clasping his two hands together in front of him. 'You disappoint me! You do not usually see things so literally!'

Charlie suddenly felt small. 'I've said something silly,' he thought to himself. 'As usual.' He lowered his eyes.

'There is no need to feel bad,' replied Japhet. 'Most humans see life in the same way.'

Charlie frowned as he raised his eyes to look at Japhet. 'Is he reading my mind?' he asked himself.

'Here, we know different,' continued Japhet. 'Here, we know that there is no line where a life begins or comes to an end. Whether in the afterlife, or walking on the Earth, or waiting to be born, it's all just part of life.'

'Who is *we*?' said Charlie. As he asked the question, Japhet looked over his shoulder and Charlie followed his gaze. Behind him, several others stepped silently forward, as if from nowhere. Many robed figures now lined the edges of the previously empty room and bowed their heads beneath deep hoods.

'We,' said Japhet, turning his attention back to Charlie, 'are The Guardians.'

'The Guardians?' repeated Charlie.

Japhet bowed his head.

'Guardians of what?'

'Of it all,' he replied. 'We are guardians of the records, and guardians of all life. There is nothing of a person's life we do not know. It is all recorded here.'

'So,' said Charlie, feeling even more unsure of himself. 'You know about my life?' He lowered his eyes again.

'Yes,' said Japhet gently. 'We know about your life.'

Charlie forced himself to meet Japhet's gaze, but he kept his head bowed a little.

'We know there are those who have let you down, Charlie Swain. We know there are those who have abandoned you, who have put their own desires above your own. And we know you have lost people you love.'

Charlie felt a lump in his throat and he swallowed to stop the tears coming to his eyes.

'Do you know why people do things?' asked Charlie, feeling afraid of the answer.

Japhet said nothing but slowly bowed his head once. 'We see the choices people make and what leads them to those choices, yes.'

Charlie fought the tears as he battled over whether to ask the question that wanted to come out. 'Is it me?' he whispered, barely able to form the words. 'My dad. Am I the reason?'

Japhet never took his eyes from Charlie.

Charlie looked away again, uncomfortable beneath his intense stare.

'No, Charlie.' Japhet's voice was sure and certain. 'You are not the reason.'

Charlie let out a sigh, a sense of relief mixed in with the part of him that wasn't sure whether to believe it. 'But how can I not be the reason?' he thought. 'If it's not me, then how come Dad loves his other son?'

194

'Life can be difficult,' said Japhet. 'And everyone gets hurt, just as everyone makes mistakes - it is all part of the game. But you should know, Charlie,' he continued, dropping his voice, 'that no heartache goes ignored.'

Charlie nodded and swallowed, trying to force the lump in his throat back down. Behind Japhet, the other guardians still did not move. Charlie didn't know whether it was the tears forming in his eyes, or whether it was real, but for the first time he noticed that the guardians along the walls had a gentle, white glow around them.

'Wrongs must be made right,' Japhet said to Charlie. 'And that is why you are here. You are the one who can help us right a wrong that was done long ago. Well, long ago according to your understanding of how time works anyway!'

Charlie frowned.

'You have solved the mystery you came to Egypt to solve, yes?'

'My friends and I have, yes.'

'This is good news,' said Japhet. 'So what have you learnt?'

'Ay killed Tutankhamun. He killed him so that he could be Pharaoh. Horemheb was part of the plan too.'

The guardians standing along the walls raised their heads.

Japhet smiled. 'At last,' he said. 'At last, the truth of this injustice is spoken by one who walks the Earth.'

Charlie frowned. 'If you knew the answer,' he asked, 'why did you need us to find it out?'

'We are guardians,' said Japhet. 'We watch over it all - but we cannot interfere. We can only influence things. We can but offer opportunities and try to show people the way. Whether they choose to accept an invitation is up to them. We cannot force anyone to do anything. And we cannot stop anything from happening either. Even when...'

Japhet stopped and looked fearful. He seemed unsure whether to continue.

'Even when, what?' asked Charlie.

The other guardians turned as one and looked in Charlie's direction. Beneath their deep hoods, all he could see were their mouths. Their eyes were completely concealed by the dark, blue fabric.

'Even,' continued Japhet, in a whisper, 'when The Others appear.'

It seemed to Charlie that the atmosphere in the room changed as Japhet spoke. Now the room seemed heavy and threatening. High up above them, the torch lights flickered violently and fought to stay alight. 'Who are The Others?' asked Charlie.

Japhet's eyes bore into Charlie's. 'The Others are like us,' he said. 'But whilst we seek to protect humanity, they try to corrupt it. Like us, they see everything, and can try to influence things. But whilst we offer people the opportunity to make choices that will help humanity, The Others offer choices that will lead to destruction. Whilst we seek to protect order and balance and justice, they seek to create chaos.'

Charlie felt afraid. 'Where are they?' he asked, his voice low and deliberate.

Japhet glanced around him nervously. 'They are everywhere.'

Every muscle in Charlie's body felt tense.

'That is why you are here,' said Japhet. 'Every injustice makes them stronger, but every injustice put right makes them weaker. Already you have helped to weaken them by speaking the truth about the young Pharaoh's death, but there is more to be done.'

'Like what?' asked Charlie. 'We have already risked our lives. Ay nearly caught us!'

'I am aware of that. But finding out the truth behind the Pharaoh's death is only part of your journey.'

'Then why did I have to leave my friends?' asked Charlie, raising his voice and feeling angry. 'We found out the truth about Ay together. We're a team.'

Japhet nodded. 'Indeed you are,' he said. 'And a good one.'

Charlie looked at him questioningly.

'But the next part of the journey, you must walk alone.'

Charlie felt terrified. 'Why?' he demanded. 'Why must I walk it alone?'

'Calm yourself,' said Japhet. 'There are things you do not know.'

'Then tell me,' said Charlie. He looked around him, angrily. 'I don't even know where I am!'

'I told you,' said Japhet. 'You're in the Hall of Records.'

'But where is that?' said Charlie impatiently.

'I thought you already knew that,' he replied. 'You worked out the meaning of the incantation.'

'No,' Charlie shook his head. 'I didn't,' he said. 'I thought it was talking about the Sphinx but clearly, I'm somewhere else.'

'I thought your grandfather once told you a story about this place,' replied Japhet.

Charlie stopped talking and frowned. 'Grandad?' he thought. An image of his grandad formed in his mind and he felt desperately home sick. 'I don't remember Grandad ever telling me a story about the Hall of Rec -'

Japhet looked at Charlie knowingly.

Charlie stared back at him. 'I don't believe it,' he said quietly.

Japhet still said nothing but looked at Charlie expectantly.

'We're...' Charlie stumbled over his words. 'We're *inside* the Sphinx?' he asked, knowing the answer.

'Beneath it, actually - but, yes.'

'At Giza?'

'Where else?' said Japhet, his one eyebrow raised.

Charlie looked up towards the ceiling, trying to picture what lay beyond it. Above their heads the huge stone sphinx lay out like a sentinel before the famous pyramids that rose from the desert sands. Somewhere above them was the Great Pyramid itself.

'Why am I here?' demanded Charlie, overwhelmed by all that had happened to him over the last few weeks.

'You are here to help us right a wrong,' said Japhet.

'I thought my friends and I had done that already,' replied Charlie.

'You have done part of it,' he said. 'But now you - and only you - must finish it.'

'Why?' said Charlie, his anger rising. 'Why must it be me?'

Japhet stepped a little closer to Charlie, the blue robe swaying silently as he did so. 'Do you remember what an Egyptian must do to enter the afterlife, Charlie?'

'Of course,' he replied. The question made him feel irritated. Normally, he loved showing off his knowledge of the ancient world but today he was not in the mood.

Japhet looked at him expectantly.

Charlie sighed. 'An Egyptian had to be pure of heart to enter the afterlife,' he said. 'He had to tell the gods that he had never done anything wrong or harmed anyone else. Then he had to place his heart on the goddess Maat's scales - the scales of order, and balance and justice.'

Japhet nodded encouragingly.

'If the heart balanced with the feather, its owner could enter the afterlife.'

'And if it didn't?' asked Japhet, never removing his eyes from Charlie.

'If it didn't, then the heart would be eaten by the crocodile headed god, Ammut.

Japhet nodded. 'And what did that mean?' he asked Charlie.

'It meant,' said Charlie, sighing impatiently, 'that he would no longer exist.'

'Exactly. To enter the afterlife, an Egyptian needs his heart. And to exist, he needs to keep it.'

Charlie nodded. 'I know all of this,' he said, feeling frustrated. 'What does this have to do with anything?'

'You tell me,' replied Japhet.

Charlie shrugged. 'I have no idea,' he said, irritated. 'Why are you asking me questions I don't know the answer to? This is so annoy -'

Japhet raised his eyebrows.

'He didn't have his heart,' said Charlie, as realisation dawned. 'Wennefer said they removed his heart during the embalming process.'

Japhet nodded.

'But he also said they'd most likely bury it with him in the tomb.'

'They didn't.'

'Why not?' asked Charlie. Then he answered his own question. 'They didn't just want to kill him,' he whispered, placing his hand across his mouth in shock. 'They wanted to wipe him out altogether. To make it as though he had never existed.'

'You are correct,' said Japhet. 'Without his heart the young Pharaoh has lain, trapped and lifeless, in his tomb, unable to enter the afterlife, and unable to exist. You must fix this. You, Charlie, must find his heart and give it back to him.'

'How do I do that?' cried Charlie. 'And why must it be me?'

'Because, Charlie,' said Japhet seriously, 'the one to right the wrong must be one with a connection to the Pharaoh.'

'A connection?' asked Charlie, feeling more and more confused. 'What kind of connection?' His mind was reeling. 'Do you mean because I'm interested in ancient Egypt and because I have a replica of the death mask in my bedroom?' he asked in disbelief. 'Lots of people have a connection like that!'

'No,' said Japhet. 'You misunderstand me. That is not the connection of which I speak.'

Charlie held out his hands to show he had nothing else to offer. He had no idea what Japhet was talking about.

'The connection, Charlie, must be a family one. Only one who belongs to the bloodline of Tutankhamun can seek out his heart and return it to him. It is the way of things. A blood relative must be allowed to put right the injustice.'

'What are you talking about?' Charlie asked, unsure whether to laugh or shout. 'I'm no more a relative of Tutankhamun than I am of you!'

'You have Egyptian blood, Charlie.'

'So what?' said Charlie, not believing a word. 'And in any case,' he said, feeling triumphant, 'Tutankhamun's children never survived - so how can he have any living relatives today?' Charlie puffed out his chest, confident that he had outwitted Japhet in whatever game this was.

Japhet's voice was certain. 'You are correct in what you say, Charlie,' he said. 'Tutankhamun's children died in infancy.'

'Exactly,' said Charlie, feeling defiant. 'I'm ready to go home.'

'Tutankhamun died without an heir,' said Japhet. 'But his siblings had children. You, Charlie, through your grandfather's line, are a descendent of Tutankhamun's half sister, Meritaten, who was a daughter of Tutankhamun's father, Akhenaten, and his wife, Nefertiti. Meritaten was also the sister of Tutankhamun's wife, Ankhesenamun. You, Charlie, are one of her descendants. That is why it must be you.'

As Charlie listened, the guardians lining the walls lifted their hoods from their heads. Each one of them stared intently towards him. In that moment, he knew he was hearing the truth.

'I can't,' said Charlie. 'I wouldn't know what to do.'

'You can,' said Japhet. 'You must trust.'

'But what do I need to do?' asked Charlie, fear gripping him. His chest felt tight and he was finding it difficult to breathe.

'You must go out onto the Giza plateau. You must go out into the desert above us...and you will find the way. It will be shown to you.'

Charlie looked at them, all staring back at him, and he felt panic. 'I can't,' he said.

'You can,' replied Japhet. 'If you choose not to do this, the injustice will continue to be, and The Others will grow stronger. Restore Tutankhamun's heart to him, Charlie. Allow him to exist again. Let him live again in the afterlife as he should always have been allowed to do.'

Charlie's mind was racing. He didn't want to let chaos win out, and he wanted to help Tutankhamun, but he was terrified. Then he had a thought. 'You said all of these books are a record of every life?' he asked, pointing to the shelves.

'That's right, yes.'

'Then everyone alive has a book here?'

'Everyone alive, and everyone who has ever lived, has a book here. And those waiting to be born have a blank book, ready to be filled.'

'Is the book you gave me *my* book?' asked Charlie.

'No. That is but a small part of your life's story. That book was to help you.'

'Then can I see my book?' Charlie asked.

'Why?' asked Japhet. 'You already know your story.'

'I want to know what's going to happen.'

'Why?'

'So that I can know whether it will work out alright.'

Japhet smiled gently. 'It doesn't work that way, Charlie. You must make your choices without knowing how they will turn out.'

'But you are asking me to step into the unknown - alone! Don't I deserve to know what's going to happen?'

'No one ever knows for certain what will happen, Charlie. You just have to make your choice. That is the great gift of humanity. You are always free to choose.'

Charlie glared at him.

'In any case,' he said. 'Imagine how boring life would be if you knew how everything was going to turn out before you even tried it.' His voice became stronger, the way Charlie remembered it when he had told him to take the book, back in the shop. 'As ever, Charlie, the choice is yours. But it is time to make it. Will you help the young Pharaoh?'

Charlie rubbed his eyes and sighed before casting his eyes up at the ceiling. In spite of what Japhet said, he didn't really feel he had a choice. He said nothing, but simply nodded.

Japhet nodded in return. 'It is time,' he said, looking to the others behind him. Then he turned back to Charlie. 'We will be watching, Charlie. And you will be shown the way.' His eyes were intense.

Charlie looked back at him and hoped he had made the right choice.

'And don't forget: beware of The Others. They are everywhere, and they will do everything they can to stand in your way. You must find it in yourself to believe.'

'Believe,' thought Charlie, as he remembered what the book had said when he and his friends had been wondering how they'd get home. Charlie thought about home, and about his friends sat somewhere hiding from Ay, and the fear became too much. 'We have done enough,' he said. 'We need to go home. The book said we had to believe it would reveal the incantation. And we have believed in it. Now it's only fair that it keeps its end of the bargain and tells us how to get home!'

Japhet sighed. 'Oh, Charlie,' he said. 'The book did say to believe but it didn't mean that you were to believe in the book to light the way.'

Charlie looked at him with a mixture of fear and confusion.

'No,' said Japhet, shaking his head. 'The book was telling you to believe in *yourself*.'

'In *me*?' asked Charlie, in disbelief.

'Of course,' said Japhet. 'Before he can achieve anything, a hero must first believe in himself.'

Charlie couldn't believe what he was hearing. 'So we can't get home?' he asked, his tone accusing.

'Of course you can,' said Japhet, his voice calm and even. 'But first you must finish what you came here to do.'

'So now it's all on me?' Charlie was almost shouting now. 'I have to do this alone? And I have to do it right if my friends and I are to go home?'

'Yes,' said Japhet. 'You do.'

Charlie dropped his shoulders and sighed deeply. 'Then we're in trouble,' he thought.

CHAPTER TWENTY-ONE

Charlie realised with horror he was no longer in the Hall of Records with The Guardians. Instead, he was lying down with his eyes closed, and he had no clue how long he had been there. He opened his eyes and squinted against the light of the sun. Slowly, he rubbed his hand suspiciously over the ground beneath him. It was sand. And it was hot and dry, nothing like the sand on the beach his mom took him to last summer. That sand had been cool and wet, soaked by the crashing waves. There was no sound of waves where Charlie now lay.

Closing his eyes tight again he tried to recall how he had got there. In his mind, he could just make out a fuzzy image of The Guardians. In the image, they all moved towards him as a group, the palms of their right hands held out towards him, as they chanted something as one. That was the last thing he remembered before opening his eyes, and quite how he had got here was a blur.

As he lay there, Charlie felt something fall on his forehead, and he wiped it away with the back of his hand. He opened his eyes again and used his hand to shield them from the burning glare of the sun. Then he felt something fall onto his forehead again. This time he wiped it away with his fingers, and managed to sit up. 'What is that?' he asked himself. He could feel the heat of the sun beating down on his head, a heat mirrored by that of the sand beneath his legs. Feeling uncomfortable, he looked down at his fingers as he felt yet another drop of something fall onto him, this time on top of his head. It felt wet, like raindrops. 'It can't be raining in the desert,' he said, as his eyes focused on his fingers and a look of horror crossed his face. He looked down in disbelief, unsure what to do. Between his fingers, he had smeared a red, sticky substance. 'Is that -' More of the red substance fell from the sky and soon the single droplets had turned into a deluge, covering him in splatters of red. 'It's blood!' yelled Charlie in horror, standing to his feet and starting to run, although he had no idea where he was going.

Some way away, behind him and to his left, the Sphinx carried out its watch, apparently unaware of Charlie's panic. In the distance ahead, three pyramids rose, tall and imposing from out of the sand that was now turning a shade of reddish pink as the drops continued to fall from the sky. Stretching out along the sand, and heading towards each of the pyramids, were long causeways, each one framed by walls, and each with archways at intervals along it. Charlie made a decision and headed for the nearest archway. He ran as fast as he could, the sand slowing him down as his feet sank into it with each stride.

Charlie reached the archway and sheltered beneath it, doing his best to keep as close to the wall as he could, but as he did, the red liquid stopped falling. Charlie looked down at his clothes, staring at the splatters of blood that covered them. 'What is going on here?' Charlie asked himself, feeling lonely and afraid. 'I wish my friends were here.'

Charlie crouched down and leant against the wall, feeling lost and not knowing what to do next. As he sat there, trying to make himself feel calmer, he heard a noise. It was quiet at first, a small but familiar noise from somewhere to his right. Charlie looked around and heard it again, and then again. 'I know that sound,' Charlie said to himself, trying to place it. And then it became clear.

He just saw one at first. A small, green creature with long back legs and bulbous eyes leapt towards him un- threateningly, it's ribbit sound greeting him. Charlie frowned, trying to work out if it was normal to see a frog in the desert. Then he heard the same sound, louder this time, over to his left, and Charlie recoiled in horror. 'Oh, my...'

Charlie stood up and ran again. He ran as fast as he could along the causeway, out from beneath the archway and heading anywhere that would take him away from what followed. Behind him, thousands upon thousands of frogs leapt in his direction. Their combined sound so loud it was deafening.

And then things got worse. As he ran, Charlie became aware of a buzzing sound to accompany the sound of the frogs. He managed to look over his shoulder as he ran, and he began to scream. As the frogs followed him along the ground, swarms of flies now followed him in the air, their buzz as loud as the noise made by the frogs, and their number partly blotting out the daylight.

'You said you'd be watching!' yelled Charlie above the din. 'You said I'd be shown the way!' He ran as fast as he could and saw a break up ahead in the causeway wall. The stones had broken away, either a natural result of their age, or because someone had broken through them. Ei- ther way, Charlie saw his opportunity and headed for it. 'Help me!' he yelled out to The Guardians. 'Please, help me!'

As he finished yelling, his voice barely audible above the noise of the frogs and flies that followed, he dived through the gap in the causeway wall and behind a nearby tomb. Under the shadow of the pyramids, the tomb stood amongst many others just like it, but these tombs were, unlike the pyramids, small and flat and rectangular. It was a good hiding place and Charlie watched in relief as the frogs and flies followed him through the break in the causeway wall and headed onwards, jumping and flying right past the tomb where Charlie now stood, and out into the endless desert beyond.

Charlie threw himself onto the floor, his back leaning against the tomb, and tried to catch his breath. As he did, he looked out over the sand, willing the frogs and flies to keep going. He refused to take his eyes from them until they had become little more than a dot in the distance. 'What do I do now?' he asked himself, as he stood up again and started to look around him.

On any other day, in any other circumstances, Charlie would have been amazed by where he now stood. His feet sank into desert sand, the Egyptian sun blazed down, and there in front of him, rising endlessly up into the cloudless, blue sky, was the famous tomb of the Pharaoh Khufu - the Great Pyramid itself. But the fear and the urgency of his situation, along with the strangeness of being chased by a mass of frogs and flies, had left Charlie numb to all sense of excitement. Instead, all he could do was think about what Japhet had said to him. 'The Others,' he whispered to himself, certain that they were behind the blood and the frogs and the flies.

He looked around him, feeling empty. Behind him, and to his right, he could still see the Sphinx, its back turned dismissively towards him, and to his left, Khafre's pyramid looked back at him, with Menkaure's pyramid beyond. Smaller pyramids also stood silently in the sand, and many more of the flat, rectangular tombs were nearby. In the distance, Charlie could also see the workmen's village, the homes and workshops of the many who had worked together to make these huge buildings possible.

And then he saw it. From somewhere near the top of the Great Pyramid, it started as a slight gleam at first, and then it grew brighter, like a mirror reflecting the sun. From up above it blinked down at Charlie, its brightness blinding.

'That must be it!' said Charlie, feeling a little relieved that he was being shown the way as promised. 'That must be the way!' And with a new sense of determination to accompany his constant fear, Charlie started to climb the side of the Great Pyramid.

CHAPTER TWENTY-TWO

The three friends fell to the ground with a thump. Clouds of dry sand flew up around them and then landed in their eyes and hair.

'Paige rubbed her eyes and coughed. 'I know The Guardians told us to prepare ourselves but that was worse than travel through the portal!'

Sheena sat in the sand and nodded. 'I think I'm going to be sick. Do you have any water, George?'

George didn't answer.

'George?'

Whilst the two girls were still sitting on the sand, George had stood up and was staring past them, transfixed, his mouth open.

'George?' said Sheena again. She turned to Paige, 'What's wrong with him?'

George put his hand onto the tops of their heads and turned them to look over their shoulders. Still, he didn't speak.

As they looked behind them, Sheena and Paige also fell silent, and slowly, with their eyes firmly fixed on the landscape, they too rose to their feet.

The whole of the Giza plateau stretched out before them. Just ahead, slightly to their left, the Sphinx gazed back at them silently, refusing to give up its secrets. Its giant paws reached out towards them and, with its head held proudly aloft, it looked out into the distance. Behind it, three long pathways with walls either side of them ran up to the three giant pyramids that dominated the landscape, their peaks reaching up towards the sun. There were smaller pyramids too, and much smaller, rectangular shaped tombs clustered together to form a cemetery. In the distance was a whole village. And beyond it all, was the endless desert.

'Look at this place,' said George finally, in amazement. 'We're standing at Giza!'

'I can't believe this,' said Sheena, her voice filled with awe.

Beside her, Paige simply shook her head in disbelief. 'Look how big this place is,' she said. And then, reminding them all why they were there, she said, 'How will we ever find Charlie in a place so huge?'

Their mood changed from wonder to concern, and the little group fell silent again, each lost in their own thoughts.

'I thought this would be such an adventure,' said Sheena. 'But now I'm afraid we'll never get home.'

'We'll get home,' said George, his voice filled with certainty.

'How can you be so sure?' asked Sheena.

'Because Charlie will make sure of it,' said George.

Sheena nodded gently. 'You're right.'

'I agree,' said Paige. 'I believe in Charlie to get us home.'

'The question is,' said Sheena, 'how can we help Charlie?'

'Let's start by finding him,' said George. 'Then we can decide how to help.'

The little group started to walk forwards, their feet sinking into the sand. Finally, they reached the Sphinx and then headed past it, deeper into the endless buildings and tombs of Giza.

'I thought the Sphinx had lost its beard,' said Paige, staring up at the creature as they walked past it, and up at the beard that was clearly intact.

'It has,' agreed George. 'A fragment of it's in the British Museum.'

'Well it has it now,' said Sheena, looking up.

'Then what time period are we in?' said Paige, sounding confused. 'The Guardians made it seem as though Tutankhamun had been murdered so long ago. I thought maybe we were back in the present day. But how can we be, if the Sphinx still has its beard?'

George shook his head. 'I have no idea what time we're in,' said George. 'Let's just find Charlie.'

As they headed onwards, Paige frowned. 'Something's not right,' she said, looking out into the desert.

'What do you mean?' asked Sheena.

'The sand looks a weird, pinkish colour,' said Paige. 'And look - there's a dead frog. And there's another one!' she said, pointing further away. 'And there, too! They're everywhere.'

'You're right,' said George. 'Not that anything that's happened so far is normal,' he continued, 'but this all feels really weird.'

'Ow!' said Sheena suddenly. 'What's that?'

'Ow!' said George.

'What's going on?' yelled Paige as one of the large, white stones falling from the sky hit her right in the middle of the forehead.

'Run!' yelled George, as they ran towards the long causeway that led to one of the pyramids. 'Head for that archway!'

They all started to run. 'What's happening?' yelled Sheena.

'It's hailing!' said George.

'Hailing?' shouted Sheena. 'In the desert? In Egypt?'

'It's definitely hail!' yelled George. 'And the stones are big!'

They finally reached the archway as hailstones the size of golf balls pelted down from the sky, hurting whomever they hit and making a loud clattering noise as they fell.

'Is this normal?' asked Paige.

'No,' said George. 'It's definitely not normal.'

'Maybe it's The Others?' suggested Sheena, her eyes wide in fear. 'The Guardians said to be careful of The Others.'

'I think maybe you're right,' said Paige. 'Nothing will stop you getting things done like huge hailstones raining down on you. Maybe they're trying to slow us down?'

'Maybe they're trying to stop us from getting to Charlie altogether?' suggested Sheena.

And then the hail stopped, just as suddenly as it had started.

'Or maybe not,' said Sheena, clearly relieved that the hail had ended.

'Shhh, can you hear that?' asked George.

They all stopped and listened.

'Hear what?' asked Paige.

It started almost like a gentle rattle, just some noise in the distance. But then it grew louder.

'That!' said George as they all looked at one another in fear.

'What is it?' asked Sheena, the sound growing louder as it moved ever closer.

'Oh, my -' George didn't finish the sentence.

Something large and dark headed their way. It looked like some kind of black cloud, but the cloud was alive as the thousands of smaller parts that formed it moved within it.

'What is that?' asked Paige.

The three of them stared. George's mouth was hanging open.

'Get down!' yelled George. 'They're heading this way!'

Paige and Sheena joined George in screaming as they crouched down near to the ground. Soon the sound surrounded them, so loud they could barely hear one another shouting, and above them, the cause of the sound blotted out the sun.

'What is it?' yelled Paige, distraught.

'I don't know!' Sheena shouted back.

'It's locusts!' yelled George. 'Thousands of them!'

Finally, the sound died down and the three friends cautiously raised up from their crouching position.

'Where did they come from?' asked Sheena, her face filled with terror.

Paige responded by smacking her hand on Sheena's arm.

'Ow!' Sheena exclaimed. 'What was that for?'

'You had a locust on your arm,' replied Paige, shuddering. 'It was massive.'

'Ew!' said Sheena. 'Has it definitely gone?'

'It's gone,' said Paige.

'Are you sure? I feel like it's still on me.'

'It's definitely gone. Are you ok, George?'

The two girls looked at George who was sitting silently with his back against the wall, looking deep in thought.

'George?' said Paige again.

'Hmm?'

'Are you ok?' asked Sheena.

'I'm not sure,' he replied. 'We're ok for the moment, but I've got a feeling we won't be in a minute.'

'Why?' asked Paige, the dread in her voice mirrored by the look of horror on Sheena's face.

'The sand was pinkish in colour, and we saw dead frogs when we arrived,' he said to them.

Paige and Sheena nodded in agreement.

'And since we've been here, it's hailed and there's just been a plague of locusts.'

'That's right,' agreed Sheena.

George looked at them intently. 'It's the plagues of Egypt,' he said.

Paige only whispered. 'You think The Others have sent the plagues of Egypt?'

'I do, yes.'

Sheena put her forehead in her hand. 'Oh, no,' she said. 'Weren't there ten of those?'

'Yes,' said George. 'But we must've missed some of them. Locusts is number eight. Just be grateful we turned up at hail - immediately before that it's boils.'

'Ew,' said Sheena again. 'I do not want boils.'

'My thoughts exactly,' agreed George. 'We should get out from under this archway and try to find Charlie while we still can. If I remember right, the next plague is darkness, and if that comes it will be even harder to find him.'

Together, they made their way back out onto the sand, the pyramids towering above them.

'Where is he?' asked Sheena, clearly worried.

'I don't know,' said George, his own voice filled with concern.

'There!' said Paige, sounding ecstatic. 'There's someone on the pyramid! Look! That's him!'

'You're right!' agreed Sheena. 'It's him!'

'What is he doing?' asked George, staring up at the pyramid.

Beside him, Sheena pointed at its very tip. 'There's something up there,' she said. 'Look!'

Paige and George looked in the direction that Sheena was pointing and saw a light reflecting back at them.

'Is that what he's heading for?' asked Paige.

'Try to get his attention,' said Sheena. 'We need to let him know we're here to help him.'

From far below, the three friends shouted as loud as they could. 'Charlie!' they yelled, waving their hands and jumping around, trying to get him to notice them. 'Charlie!'

For a second it seemed as though Charlie had heard them, and from where they stood it appeared as though he looked briefly in their direction. But in that instant, the sun stopped shining and the skies turned black, plunging the desert into darkness.

In the blackness, the three friends stopped shouting and looked around them at the new sound heading their way. It started as a hiss, the sound of a thousand snakes in the desert, and then sand began swirling up and surrounding them, accompanied by the sound of a fierce, whistling wind. In the same moment, a loud rumble echoed around the desert and a fork of lightning streaked its way across the sky.

'They've sent a storm,' said George. 'He'll never hear us now.'

Overhead, the sky crashed and banged and the lightning crackled and lit up the world with its silver flashes.

'So this is number nine?' asked Sheena.

'Yes,' nodded George. 'This is number nine.'

'But there are ten?'

'Yes,' replied George, his gaze fixed on the Great Pyramid where Charlie was climbing ever upwards.

'So what's number ten?' asked Paige.

At first, George didn't reply.

'George,' said Paige again urgently. 'What's number ten?'

Sheena and Paige stared at him intently but George never took his eyes from the pyramid.

Slowly, as the storm raged overhead, he answered. 'It's death,' he said.

CHAPTER TWENTY-THREE

The place around Charlie was dark. It smelt damp and musty. Somewhere over to the left he could hear the endless drip of water, the droplets making a tapping sound as they fell onto a solid surface. As his eyes adjusted to the gloom, he could just make out the shapes of stalactites hanging above his head, close enough to have caused real damage had he been taller. They pointed threateningly down at him, like daggers. Occasionally, a trickle of water ran down one of them and fell onto his hair. Beneath his feet, the ground was hard and uneven, its rocky surface slippery in places. He slipped a little and fought hard to control his footing, realising almost too late that he was standing right on the edge of some kind of bank. Immediately in front of him, it gave way to a huge body of water. In the dimness, he couldn't tell if it was a river or a lake but he could tell that it was motionless.

'Where am I?' Charlie asked himself, feeling afraid. He looked around for any other sign of life but there was none. 'I'm alone,' he thought. 'I'm completely alone in this place. And I don't know where I am or how to get out.'

Then he heard another sound. It was distant at first, so quiet he might not have heard it were it not for the fact that the water had begun to move gently. Then it grew louder. The water began to slap violently against the side of the bank, its sound accompanied by a second noise, a sort of swishing sound, as if something were moving in and out of the water. And then he saw it. A long, wooden boat appeared as if from nowhere and headed towards him. At its stern stood a tall figure, dressed in a long cloak and moving the boat forward with an oar that he moved from side to side. He seemed to pay no attention to Charlie, but occasionally looked back over his shoulder in the direction from which the boat had come.

Charlie watched the boat, afraid. Eventually its bow reached the bank and the boat stopped. It pointed towards the bank and bobbed up and down on the water.

For the first time, the boatman looked at Charlie. His eyes seemed to glow, the only hint of brightness anywhere. 'Who awaits the ferryman?' asked the boatman, his voice echoing around them.

Charlie didn't answer. He tried to move but he felt glued to the spot, fear gripping him.

The boatman stared back at him, silent. The dripping water seemed suddenly deafening.

'What is your purpose?' asked the boatman, speaking for the second time. 'What is your purpose here?' The boatman sounded angry and impatient.

'I don't know,' said Charlie, forcing himself to speak.

'You don't know?' replied the boatman, his anger growing. 'Then why did you wake me?' he boomed, the echoes growing louder.

'I didn't wake you,' said Charlie. 'I don't know who you are. I don't even know where this is.' He swallowed. 'It must be someone else who woke you.'

The boatman stared at Charlie and then began to laugh. It was a loud laugh, so loud that Charlie felt the ground beneath his feet shake. Finally, the laugh stopped, and the boatman's toothless mouth twisted into a cruel grin.

'Every so often one comes along like you,' he said, apparently enjoying himself. 'One who has no idea where he is or how he got here.' He laughed again, leaning on his oar. The boat continued to sway in the water but the boatman kept his perfect balance. 'Allow me to enlighten you,' he said, finally. 'You are in the underworld. The afterlife,' he clarified. 'You are in the land of the dead.'

'The land of the dead?' asked Charlie, finding it difficult to breathe.

The boatman simply bowed his head in agreement.

'But, how did I get here?' asked Charlie.

The boatman laughed again, and this time the laugh seemed to go on forever. It echoed all around Charlie and made the whole place shake.

'Ah, denial,' said the boatman, finally calming himself. 'That's my favourite!'

Charlie looked back at the boatman, feeling hurt.

'There is only one way to get to the land of the dead,' said the boatman, clearly taking pleasure from delivering the news. 'You have to die.'

Charlie felt more afraid than he had ever felt in his life. He thought about his friends and about home and about his mom and his grandad. 'You mean, I'm...'

'Yes,' said the boatman, all hint of a smile gone from his face. 'You're dead.'

Charlie could do or say nothing. He wanted to go home.

'I'm impatient,' said the boatman. 'I don't enjoy being woken. It's my job to take you across the river,' he said. 'But first you must tell me what you intend to do here.'

Charlie thought, his mind racing. 'Am I really dead?' he asked himself. He looked down at his hands, to see if he was still there. Although the light was dim, he was sure he could make out the outline of his hands, and his feet too. He touched his right hand with his left, and then his left with his right. They felt solid. 'I don't feel dead,' he thought.

'And yet, you are,' said the boatman.

Charlie looked at him in surprise.

'There are no secrets here,' said the boatman. 'This is the land of the dead, you cannot hide your thoughts, and you cannot hide your deeds. Here, all will be brought out into the open. And all wrongs will be put right.'

'All wrongs will be put right,' he whispered to himself, repeating the boatman's words. 'Perhaps,' he thought, remembering all Japhet had said to him, 'that's the reason I'm here.' He turned to the boatman. 'I am here to right a wrong,' he said to him. 'I am here to find Tutankhamun's heart, and to return it to him.'

As Charlie finished speaking, there was a loud, rumbling sound. The ceiling above him began to shake, just a little at first and then violently. Small pieces of rock began to fall downwards, and a stalactite lost its grip on the roof and smashed loudly on the floor.

'It seems there are those who wish to see you fail,' said the boatman, raising his voice above the din and looking upwards. 'Come,' he said, gesturing towards the bow of the boat. 'I will take you across the river.'

Charlie hesitated and then stepped onto the boat. There was no turning back.

The boatman turned the boat effortlessly around and began to row back across the river. And the din behind them stopped. Neither of them spoke again. Had he not felt so frightened, the rhythmic sound of the oar, along with the gentle rocking of the boat, would have made Charlie fall fast asleep.

'We're here,' said the boatman, pulling the boat alongside another bank.

Charlie stepped off the boat onto ground that was flat and solid, unlike the ground back on the other side. Here it was also bright and airy, as if the sun were shining down. Charlie found this side of the river to be much more agreeable than the other side. He turned to thank the ferryman, but he wasn't there. Instead of the river with the boat that had brought him across the water, there was nothing but a large, open field. The river, like the ferryman, had disappeared.

Charlie looked around him. The field was full of tall grass but he could still see over it. All around, he caught glimpses of other people. Some looked a lot like him, solid and real, but others were little more than grey shadows. None of them paid him any attention. Except one. From the other side of the field, a figure made its way over to him. Her dress swished as she walked, and as she came nearer, Charlie realised he recognised her.

'Grandma!' he exclaimed, throwing himself into her arms. 'Is that really you?' Charlie had never felt so happy and so relieved in his whole life.

'Hello, my Charlie!' she replied, smiling broadly and hugging him tight. 'It's so good to see you - but there isn't much time. You don't belong here.'

'But the boatman said I was dead, Grandma.'

She smiled at him kindly, cupping his face in her hands. 'You're more in between,' she said. 'And you need to go back. It's not your time to die.'

Charlie remembered what the boatman had said about not being able to keep secrets here, and he lowered his voice to a whisper. 'I have to find Tutankhamun's heart,' he said.

His grandma nodded. 'I know,' she said. 'I'm going to help you. The underworld can be a dangerous place if you don't know what you're doing. Here,' she said, handing him a scroll.

'What is it, Grandma?' Charlie asked her, taking the scroll.

'It's the Book of the Dead,' she replied, and Charlie looked down at the scroll in disbelief. 'In it is everything you will need to get through the underworld safely - but first, you have to pass the Weighing of the Heart Ceremony.'

Charlie stared at her. 'I have to go through the Weighing of the Heart Ceremony?'

She nodded. 'If you want to go further into the land of the dead and find Tutankhamun's heart, yes.'

Charlie felt his heart sink. He knew what that ceremony meant. 'But my heart could be thrown to Ammut,' he said, feeling terrified. 'If she eats my heart, I won't just be dead - I won't even exist!'

His grandma placed a hand on each of his shoulders. 'You will pass the test,' she said. 'The Guardians chose you, Charlie, for a reason.'

'They said they chose me because it must be a relative of the Pharaoh who returns his heart to him.'

'That's true,' replied his grandma. 'But it's more than that. They also needed someone whose heart was pure. Someone whose heart would pass the test without having to cheat.'

'You can cheat?' asked Charlie in disbelief. 'I thought the gods knew everything?'

'No one knows everything, Charlie. And yes, you can cheat. But if you cheat, you doom yourself to live in darkness and misery. You may be able to cheat others, even the gods themselves, but you cannot cheat yourself.'

'But I've made mistakes, Grandma. What if my heart won't balance with the feather?'

'Lovely boy!' she said. 'It is not our genuine mistakes that weigh down our hearts! It's when we intentionally cause harm that it makes us less than we are. You have been hurt Charlie, but you have not let it destroy you. You continue to be kind, even though others may not be so kind to you. You do not need to cheat. And that is why The Guardians chose you.'

Charlie looked into his grandma's familiar and kind eyes.

'I'll meet you on the other side,' she said.

'Other side?'

She nodded. 'I'll meet you on the other side of that door,' she said, pointing out a door he was sure hadn't been there before.

'You're not coming with me?'

'Some things, we must do alone,' she replied, and then she was gone.

CHAPTER TWENTY-FOUR

Charlie looked around him but his grandma was nowhere to be seen. When he looked back around, he was standing right in front of the door she had pointed out to him. 'How did I get this close?' he wondered.

The door, or rather the double doors, were huge. Made of a dark wood, they towered above Charlie. He looked at the spot where a handle should be, but there was none. Instead, he took a deep breath and knocked slowly on the door. The dull noise echoed back at him, and at first nothing else happened. Then the doors swung open, inviting Charlie to step through. When he did, his feet tapping on the tiled, golden floor, they slammed loudly shut behind him.

Charlie could see he was standing at the beginning of a long, corridor-like room. The walls were covered in endless images of the gods, all of them watching him intently. From the ceiling, the goddess Maat, her wings outstretched and the feather of truth in her hair, looked down upon him. Torches, flickering their fiery light, brought a reddish glow to the room. At the far end of the room, Charlie could see a set of giant, golden scales, the pathway to them lined by around forty beings, all looking towards him. 'They are gods,' Charlie realised, as he remembered all he had read about ancient Egypt. 'This is the Weighing of the Heart Ceremony.' Fear and awe battled together for control of his mind.

At the near end of the scales stood Anubis, the large eyes of his jackal's head gleaming. Anubis said nothing but beckoned Charlie forward with his hand. Even though

Charlie knew Anubis was a protector of the dead, he had always felt fearful of Anubis. Now, more than ever, he understood why. He towered above Charlie, and his flickering shadow on the wall loomed, dark and imposing, over the whole room.

Not far from Anubis, another figure in a tall, white headdress, sat in a large, golden chair and watched over the whole thing. 'Osiris,' said Charlie in disbelief.

Taking a deep breath, Charlie stepped forward as Anubis had asked him to do. He could feel his legs shaking. A few steps later and he had begun to walk the path to the scales. The gods that lined the way fixed their eyes on him and then one of them held out their hand abruptly. Charlie stopped just as suddenly, afraid of what was about to happen.

'Have you ever intentionally harmed another?' asked the god.

Charlie could feel the weight in the air as every being in the room looked at him expectantly. Anubis held his head high and watched with clear interest.

'No,' answered Charlie, honestly.

The god held his gaze and then, apparently happy with Charlie's answer, he dropped his arm and allowed Charlie to continue forward.

Charlie took a few more steps and another of the gods did the same thing, but this time asking a different question.

'Have you ever used violence against another?'

'No,' said Charlie, and he was allowed to step forward.

'Have you ever killed anyone?' asked another.

'Have you ever cheated anyone?' asked the next.

'No,' replied Charlie, over and over again. 'I have not.'

Eventually, Charlie reached Anubis, who greeted him without speaking and placed huge hands on his shoulders, guiding him into place so that he was standing right in front of the golden scales. To Charlie they looked as tall as a building. Their central pivot rose up high into the air, and a baboon sat on top of it, looking down on Charlie and watching everything. In the right hand pan, lay a single, white feather, the feather that would decide whether he was worthy. He swallowed, and he fought to keep calm.

As Charlie stared at the feather, he heard a noise to his right, and looked in its direction. It was a strange noise, a sort of growling, combined with a gnashing sound. When Charlie saw what was causing it, he caught his breath in terror. Looking up at him from somewhere down below, was the head of a crocodile. Its eyes bore into Charlie's own as it opened its mouth and then snapped its jaw shut. Although its head and face were that of a crocodile, it had a lion's mane, and its chest and front legs and paws were also those of a lion. The back portion of its body was a hippopotamus. It was the strangest and most frightening creature Charlie had ever seen.

'Ammut,' he thought to himself as the beast continued with its low, terrifying growl. 'Eater of hearts and souls.'

The yellow, reptilian eyes stared greedily towards the scales.

Then Anubis came to stand before Charlie. Still he said nothing, and the hall fell completely silent. Even Ammut stopped growling. From his chair, Osiris leant forward.

To Charlie, it felt as though time had stopped. And then it happened. Anubis plunged his hands deep into Charlie's chest. Charlie looked down in shock, expecting to see blood, but instead Anubis' arms had passed through

Charlie's body as easily as if he had been made of water. He felt a strange sensation as the hand of the god clasped his heart, its beat becoming faster and the sound drumming in his ears. Then, without warning, Anubis withdrew his hands and held Charlie's heart in his hands. Charlie looked at it in panic, and then placed his own hand to his chest. The thumping of his heart was no longer in his ears, but now its rhythmic beat filled the room.

Charlie could do nothing but watch. Anubis held Charlie's heart up high in the air for all in the room to see. Its veins and arteries were clearly visible and even though it had been removed from Charlie's body, it kept beating.

Charlie tried to scream, but no sound would come out, and instead he heard it only inside his own head. The scream mixed in with the deafening sound of his heart beat.

Then Anubis placed his heart gently down onto the left hand pan of the scales and stepped back. Every god in the room fixed their gaze on the scales. Ammut kept her eyes on Charlie's heart.

At first the scales moved to the left, as Anubis placed the heart down. Charlie felt himself gasp. 'It's too heavy,' he thought. But then the scales moved back to centre for a moment before falling a little to the left again. The scales moved for what felt like forever. 'What if I don't pass?' he said to himself, horrified at the thought. He glanced over to Ammut, who was waiting, hungrily.

Then the scales finally came to a stop. The left pan moved upwards and came to rest alongside the pan with the feather. And then the scales stopped moving altogether. Charlie's heart had balanced perfectly.

Anubis bowed his head towards Charlie and then lifted the heart back from the scales, before plunging his hands back into Charlie's chest and removing them again, this time without Charlie's heart. Charlie felt the familiar thumping leave the room and return to his ears, the beat beginning to slow a little as he felt relief flow through him.

Then there was a loud bang as another set of double doors flung open. Charlie looked at Anubis who gestured with his hand towards the doors. Charlie was free to go.

Anubis bowed his head once more and Charlie gratefully headed towards the open doors. He walked past Ammut, trying not to look at her but hearing her angry growls as he left with his heart intact.

He exited the doors, which slammed shut behind him, and there, as promised, stood his grandmother. He threw himself towards her, relief flooding through him once again. 'I did it, Grandma!' he said.

'I never doubted you,' she said, smiling. 'Now you are free to make your way through the underworld. But act quickly, Charlie. It's almost time for you to leave.'

'Then I'll definitely go home again?' he asked.

'If you act quickly, yes,' she said. 'You don't belong here.'

CHAPTER TWENTY-FIVE

'You must go ahead alone,' Charlie's grandmother said to him. 'I have given you all you need to make it through safely,' she said, pointing at the scroll in Charlie's hand. 'If you need to know anything, just open the scroll. It's all in there.'

'Can't you come with me?' asked Charlie, almost pleading. 'I don't want to be alone here.'

'You may go on your own,' she said, 'but you aren't really alone. None of us ever is.'

Charlie looked at his grandma, feeling afraid.

'I'll find you again before it's time to go,' she said to him, hugging him tightly. 'For now, just focus on what needs to be done.'

'But I don't know what to do,' said Charlie. 'Where do I start?'

'Have a little more faith, Charlie. You've made it this far.'

Charlie felt his shoulders drop. He was so tired.

'Tell me why you're here,' she said.

'I'm here to find Tutankhamun's heart, and to return it to him,' replied Charlie. 'But I don't know how.'

'Yes, you do,' said his grandma. Her face was serious. 'Think. Where will you find his heart?'

Charlie shook his head. 'I'm not sure.'

'What happened to his heart, Charlie?'

Charlie thought back to all that had happened at the royal palace. He thought about his friends, and about

Wennefer. 'Wennefer said it was removed when Tutan-khamun was mummified,' he said. 'Wennefer assumed it would be buried with him, but it never was.'

'Why not?' asked his grandma.

'Because he cannot exist without it.'

'And who would want him to meet that fate?'

'Ay - and probably Horemheb,' replied Charlie. 'But it was Ay who killed him. I think Ay has his heart.'

His grandma nodded. 'Then you need to find Ay,' she said.

'But he could be anywhere. I don't even know what time we're in anymore. Ay could still be on Earth, ruling Egypt.'

His grandma looked at him intently. 'Ay is here,' she said.

'In the underworld?'

'Yes,' she said. 'But he is not in the Field of Reeds.'

'The Field of Reeds?'

His grandma nodded. 'That's where many go who pass the Weighing of the Heart Ceremony. But that is not where Ay has gone.' She lowered her voice. 'He passed the test because he used spells from the Book of the Dead to trick the gods, but he could not trick himself.'

'Then where do I find him?' asked Charlie, frowning.

'Go through there,' she said, pointing him in the direction of another door he had not seen before. 'But be careful,' she said. 'It's a dark place.' She looked around her and whispered, 'It's where The Others like to visit.'

'Is he there because he is being punished?' asked Charlie, whispering in return.

'In a way,' said his grandma. 'But not by the gods, or by anyone else. Though he tricked the gods, Ay's heart knows what he has done. It's his own conscience that keeps him...there.'

Charlie's grandma pointed back towards the door and Charlie looked in the direction of her finger. Beyond the field in which they now stood, the skies were a grey, swirling mass of gathering storm clouds. And beneath them, was a tall, grey door.

'I'm afraid,' he said, turning back to his grandma. But once more, she was gone.

Feeling a lump in his throat, Charlie resigned himself to his fate and headed towards the door. The warmth that had surrounded him moments before was replaced with an icy chill as he approached. When he arrived, he realised he was no longer alone. Outside of the door stood a tall, grotesque figure. His twisted, human body was hunched over and made all the more threatening by the long, dark cloak that fell from his shoulders. His gruesome head was that of vulture and a long, curved beak extended from his raw, pink flesh. From beneath his cloak, a scorpion-like tail snaked around him, the sting on the end occasionally darting forwards. In each gnarled hand, he held a razor-sharp knife, the blades as grey as the gathering clouds overhead. The creature looked at Charlie from beneath deep set, soulless, black eyes. His glare was terrifying, his features more frightening than the boatman's had been, and his growl more threatening even than that of Ammut. Way above his head, on a stone over the door, it said 'Gate Six.'

Then the creature roared. It was a noise so loud it made Charlie want to run, but fear kept him rooted to the spot. Overhead, the storm joined in, thunder crashing and lightning splitting the sky.

'Who approaches?' The cloaked figure jabbed a knife menacingly in Charlie's direction.

Charlie felt his voice waver. 'I do,' he said, trying to sound brave.

'And who are you?' bellowed the creature. 'You are no one. You have no place here. You will never cross through this gate!'

The storm whipped up into a frenzy. A fearsome wind pulled at Charlie's hair and clothes and was so strong it almost lifted him from his feet. And Charlie ran. He ran away from the storm and the wind and the bellowing creature, and decided he would run back towards the sunny field, but when he turned around, the field was gone. Instead, all was dark and stormy. He kept running anyway, and found a pile of large stones next to a small pool. He threw himself behind them, the roar of the creature at the gate still all around him. The water in the pool was as grey as the sky above.

From behind the stones, Charlie tried to catch his breath. 'Think,' he said to himself. 'What would George do?' Charlie wished with all he had that George were here now. He was so clever. 'George would have found Tutankhamun's heart by now,' he said, as the bellowing voice behind him responded.

'Indeed, he would!' boomed the voice, half laughing at him. 'A pity then, that this task has fallen to you!'

Charlie put his hands over his ears and tried to block out the sound. He bent his head down, trying to make himself as small as possible, and as he did so, he saw the scroll sticking out of his pocket. Acting quickly, he unravelled the scroll and looked for help amongst the hieroglyphs.

'Gate Six,' said a heading, some way down the scroll. Charlie felt something close to relief. 'The figure at Gate Six will try to make you doubt your own worth,' Charlie read. 'It will remind you of all your failings and will make all your doubts feel even greater. To pass through Gate Six,' it said, 'you must believe in your own worth. Any doubt, and the being will cause you great harm.'

Charlie rolled the scroll back up and threw it on the ground. 'I give up!' yelled Charlie. 'Have I not done enough?' Charlie had no idea who he was speaking to, but he shouted his frustration just the same. 'I can't do this!' he yelled out into the storm.

At that moment, the sound and winds of the storm subsided. The clouds continued to swirl violently up above, and everywhere was still a gloomy shade of grey, but around Charlie, there was only a sense of stillness and silence.

Charlie looked around him, wondering what was happening. And then the water next to him began to change. At first it became pure and glass-like, the surface of the pool looking like a mirror. And then the mirrored surface became misty and foggy and Charlie could just make out vague images moving within it. Charlie fixed his eyes on the water, willing the fogginess to clear until, finally, it did, and Charlie saw an image that made him afraid and relieved in equal measure. Charlie saw himself lying in the Egyptian sand, still and lifeless beneath the pyramids, their surfaces hazy in the desert heat. Around him were George, Paige and Sheena, all desperately trying to revive him.

Charlie couldn't believe his eyes. 'They came after me?' he asked himself.

'Come on, Charlie,' said George, pressing frantically on his chest.

'He can't be dead,' said Sheena, a tear falling down her cheek as she held Charlie's hand.

'He cannot die here!' yelled Paige, her anger causing her to kick the sand, sending a cloud of it billowing up around her.

George sat back, breathless and looking panic stricken. 'I can't revive him,' he said. 'I think he's gone.'

Sheena's eyes filled with tears, 'What?'

'We are not leaving him here,' said Paige, her anger showing no sign of subsiding.

George nodded in agreement.

'If we ever get to leave, we leave together,' said Sheena.

'Or not at all,' added George.

Charlie couldn't believe what he was seeing. His friends followed him, and now they were prepared to risk their own chances of going home for him. He bent his head nearer to the water. 'I'm here,' he yelled to them. 'I'm here!'

He watched as his three friends looked around them as if they had heard something but before Charlie could see anymore, the image changed. This time he was alive, and climbing the Great Pyramid, whilst his three friends stood together at Giza, looking for him.

'I thought this would be such an adventure,' said Sheena. 'But now I'm afraid we'll never get home.'

'We'll get home,' said George, his voice filled with certainty.

'How can you be so sure?' asked Sheena.

'Because Charlie will make sure of it,' said George.

Sheena nodded. 'You're right.'

'I agree,' said Paige. 'I believe in Charlie to get us home.'

'The question is,' said Sheena, 'how can we help Charlie?'

Then the image disappeared as quickly as it had begun. In the blink of an eye the water in the pool returned to its murky grey and the wind and sound of the storm surrounded him once more, this time even louder.

'They believed in me!' Charlie yelled through the storm. 'They believed in me!' And in that knowledge, he made a decision. Unravelling the scroll once again he headed back to the gate. The wind made it difficult to move, and with every step forward, the wind pushed back against him. Charlie leant into the wind and kept going, determined to reach the gate.

As he drew closer, the roar of the vulture headed creature grew louder. 'You dare to return?' boomed the voice. '*You*?' The creature started to laugh. It was a cruel laugh, with no sign of warmth or kindness.

Charlie stood before the figure and looked it straight in the eye. He swallowed as he tried to push down his fear and did his best to think only of his friends and all that they had said. Then he held up the scroll in front of him, and read the words it advised him to read. 'I call on the name of Anubis!' Charlie yelled, his voice barely audible above the storm and the growls. 'His is a name greater than yours! His is a name that protects me! I am here to right a wrong!' he shouted. 'And that means I am on the side of right! The gods will not allow you to harm me!' The storm was now so loud Charlie couldn't even hear himself above it. 'The gods believe in me!' he continued. 'My friends believe in me!' He paused for a moment, gathering all his courage. 'I believe in me!' he yelled. 'And I will complete this quest!' And for the first time, Charlie honestly thought he could do it. He was going to find Tutankhamun's heart, and he was going to make sure he and his friends went home.

As soon as he finished speaking, the creature let out a blood curdling shriek, like the sound of an animal caught in a trap. It squealed as though someone had pierced it through the heart with a spear, and then it was engulfed in a swirling mass of grey that moved upwards and was sucked into the storm. Then the storm stopped, and Gate Six flew open.

CHAPTER TWENTY-SIX

Feeling braver than he had ever felt in his life, Charlie stepped through the gate. 'I did it!' he said to himself, feeling proud.

Beyond the gate, Charlie had expected to see sunlight where the storm had once been, but this side was even darker and greyer. Everywhere, dull, shadow-like figures moved slowly, their heads bowed low. The landscape looked as though it had once been a field full of crops, but they had all died long ago and the dry soil was covered in rotting vegetation. The decaying plants gave off an unpleasant smell, and Charlie put his hand to his nose.

As Charlie looked around, he could see that some of the figures were more obvious than others. Some were barely visible, so faint that they were hardly there at all. Others were a deeper, darker, and somehow heavier, grey.

He walked on, wondering how to find Ay and hoping he didn't have to spend much time in this part of the underworld. 'Who would want to live here?' Charlie said aloud.

And then he heard someone crying. Stopping in his tracks and listening carefully, he followed the sound and found a woman sobbing. Unlike the others here, she was not a dark, grey shadow, but instead wore a long, light coloured gown. She sat on the floor, her legs drawn up to her chest, and her tears falling onto her knees.

Charlie stood looking at her, unsure what to do. 'Why are you crying?' he asked the woman.

She stopped and looked up in the direction of his voice, sniffing. And as she did, Charlie felt instant shock.

The woman didn't recognise him, but Charlie recognised her, and he was taken aback as he realised he was looking into the dark, teary eyes of Ankhesenamun.

'Ankhesenamun,' he whispered.

'How do you know who I am?' she asked, sounding afraid.

Charlie realised his mistake and tried to brush it away. 'You were the wife of Tutankhamun,' he said. 'Everyone knows who you are.'

Ankhesenamun stared at him, clearly wondering if he could be trusted. 'Who are you?' she asked.

Charlie decided to tell the truth. If anyone could help him, it was probably Ankhesenamun. In any case, it would help her to know she could trust him. 'I'm Charlie,' he said. 'I'm here to find Tutankhamun's heart and return it to him.'

Ankhesenamun's eyes widened. 'You're here to help my husband?'

'Yes,' said Charlie.

'Why?' she asked.

Charlie thought about how best to answer her. 'Because a great injustice was done,' he said. 'And I am here to put it right. I think Ay has his heart.'

Ankhesenamun stood up and faced Charlie. 'You know what he did?' she asked.

Charlie nodded. 'Yes,' he said. 'I do.'

'Then you know he became Pharaoh after Tutankhamun died, and you know he made me his wife?' she asked, the tears falling again.

Charlie nodded.

'But it's so much worse than that!' said Ankhesenamun. 'Ay took Tutankhamun's heart so that he would not exist even here in the underworld. And it's all my fault!'

Charlie was confused. 'Your fault?' he asked her.

She nodded and sniffed. 'Ay said he only decided to take Tutankhamun's heart when he knew I had asked a neighbouring king to send me a husband.'

'Why?' asked Charlie. 'Both Tutankhamun and the husband you asked for were dead.'

'To teach me a lesson,' she said, and she began to cry again. Then she stopped and looked Charlie straight in the eye. 'How did you know the husband I asked for died?' she whispered, her voice filled with uncertainty. 'How do you know so much?'

Charlie shook his head. 'It's not important,' he said. 'You know now why I'm here,' he continued. 'But what are you doing here, in this terrible place?'

'I don't know how to leave!' she said, crying again. 'When I died, I just ended up here. I waited and waited for Tutankhamun to come but then I found out about his heart and realised I'd never see him again. I feel so guilty,' she sobbed. 'I don't deserve to leave here!'

'Have you passed the Weighing of the Heart Ceremony?' he asked her.

She shook her head. 'No,' she said. 'I'd never pass it, not after all I've done. I am meant to stay here,' she said, looking around her and starting to cry again.

'Then how did you get this far into the afterlife?' Charlie asked her.

'I had to cheat,' she said. 'Because I knew, after everything I had done to make Ay take Tutankhamun's heart, that I would never pass. And I was too afraid to let Ammut eat my own heart, even though I deserve it,' she said. Her dark eyes filled again with tears. 'I would give anything to be able to pass it honestly.'

Charlie felt sorry for her. After everything Ay had done, he had somehow also convinced Tutankhamun's queen that she was to blame. It made Charlie angry. 'He won't get away with this,' said Charlie.

Ankhesenamun nodded gently but looked unconvinced.

Charlie thought about all his grandma had told him - that it was Ay's own conscience that kept him where he was. 'It must be the same for Ankhesenamun,' he said to himself. 'Yet she has done nothing wrong. She too needs this injustice to be put right.' He looked at her as she wiped away her tears. 'That's why she isn't grey and shadowy like the others,' he thought to himself. 'She doesn't really belong here.'

'I think I can help you,' said Charlie.

'You can help me?' she asked, a look of relief crossing her face.

'Yes,' said Charlie, 'I think I can. But first I have to find Ay.'

'Then you've come to the right place,' she sniffed.

'You know where he is?'

'Yes,' nodded Ankhesenamun with a shudder. 'Come with me,' she said. 'I'll show you.'

CHAPTER TWENTY-SEVEN

Charlie followed Ankhesenamun through dirt and mud and fields of smelly, rotting crops, before she finally came to a stop behind an old, decaying building.

'He's over there,' she said, pointing cautiously from behind the crumbling stones.

Charlie looked. Not far away, sat on the ground, cross legged and looking dirty and ragged, was the shadowy figure that was Ay. He looked nothing like he had looked when Charlie and his friends had seen him at Karnak and the royal palace. 'What is he holding in his hands?' Charlie asked Ankhesenamun, as he spotted the small jar Ay clasped tightly to his chest.

'I don't know.' Ankhesenamun shook her head. 'He won't tell me. But whatever it is, he is always carrying it. I try to stay away from him,' she said angrily.

Charlie looked again at the pot. It was dark grey and unpainted. It wasn't large but it was big enough to hold a human heart. 'I think that's it!' said Charlie.

'What?' asked Ankhesenamun.

'I think that jar has Tutankhamun's heart in it!'

'You think so?' asked Ankhesenamun, looking distraught. 'You mean all this time he has had my husband's heart and I didn't even know?'

Charlie looked at her with compassion. 'You weren't to know,' he said. 'What matters is that we put this right. Will you help me?'

Ankhesenamun sounded determined. 'Yes,' she said. 'If Ay has my husband's heart, I will help you get it back.' She looked at Charlie intently. 'But how?' she asked.

'We need to distract him.'

Together they peered out at Ay, watching him. Charlie wondered what to do next.

'Leave it to me,' said Ankhesenamun. 'I will distract him and get him to put down the jar. When you can, take it.'

'You're sure?' asked Charlie.

'Yes,' she replied. 'Anything for Tutankhamun.' She stepped out from behind the building and made her way over to Ay.

From his hiding place, Charlie could just make out what she was saying.

'Hello, Husband,' she greeted Ay, who looked up from his sitting position. He seemed surprised to see her. 'Are you not pleased to see me?' she asked him, but he only stared, his eyes looking lifeless and vacant. 'Aren't you tired of feeling so lonely?' she asked. 'I know I am. Perhaps we can make this life more pleasant, if we live it together.'

Ay remained silent, but his face showed a flicker of recognition. Ankhesenamun bent down and gently put her hands around the pot he clasped to him. She tried to take it from him but he gripped it tighter, pulling his arms in towards his chest.

'Do you not trust me, Husband?' she said to him, placing a hand on his cheek. 'Will you not take my hand? Wouldn't you rather hold my hand than a lifeless pot?'

He frowned, and she tried once more. This time, Ay reluctantly let go of the pot and she placed it by his side.

'You see,' she said. 'I only want to set it down.' She stood to her feet again. 'Take my hand,' she said, holding both hands out towards Ay. 'Let me help you to your feet.'

Slowly, uncertainly, Ay moved his hands forward and took Ankhesenamun's.

From behind the building, Charlie held his breath as he watched Ay stand to his feet, and he knew that this was his one chance. Ahead, Ankhesenamun held onto Ay and pulled him gently around so that his back was to the pot. Charlie saw his moment, and crept over to where the pot sat on the ground. When he reached it, he snatched it up into his own arms, just as Ankhesenamun snatched her hands from Ay's.

'Run!' she shouted.

Ay turned around. He was slow, but he recognised Charlie. 'You!' he said. 'It's you! You have stolen from the Pharaoh before!'

Charlie and Ankhesenamun ran.

'Which way?' she asked.

'This way!' shouted Charlie. 'Follow me!'

Charlie led Ankhesenamun back across the rotting fields towards Gate Six. Somewhere behind, Ay was following, but he was sluggish, as if living there had somehow made him a shadow of his former self.

'Quite literally,' thought Charlie.

They reached the gate, which still lay wide open, and both Charlie and Ankhesenamun threw themselves across its threshold. As they tumbled through, they turned around just in time to see Ay heading towards them, and then the gate slammed shut with a bang.

CHAPTER TWENTY-EIGHT

'We made it,' said Charlie to Ankhesenamun.

'Indeed you did,' said a voice behind him.

Charlie had expected to feel fields beneath him but instead he felt cold tile beneath his legs. He twisted around to face the voice, still gripping the jar in his hands, and looked into the face of a young man he recognised.

'Tutankhamun!' yelled Ankhesenamun joyously, leaping to her feet and throwing her arms around him. 'I thought I would never see you again!'

He hugged her back. 'Were it not for Charlie, you would not have done,' he said. He turned to Charlie. 'Thank you, my friend.'

'Then I was right?' said Charlie, proud of himself. 'It really is your heart in here?' He held up the pot as he spoke.

'So it would seem,' replied Tutankhamun.

As the Pharaoh spoke, there was a deep voice from the other end of the long, corridor-like room in which they stood. 'It is time,' it said.

Charlie looked towards the voice and saw Anubis, beckoning the young Pharaoh and Ankhesenamun forward. Gods lined a pathway up to a large set of gold scales, on which rested a single, white feather.

'I think you'll be needing this,' said Charlie, holding out the pot.

Tutankhamun took it in both hands. 'I am in your debt,' he said.

Charlie waved his hand to dismiss the idea. 'That's what family is for,' he said, smiling.

The young Pharaoh smiled back, broadly. 'Nevertheless,' he said, 'if ever you need me to return the favour...'

'I know where to find you,' replied Charlie.

Tutankhamun turned to Ankhesenamun. 'Are you ready?' he asked her.

'Me?' she asked. 'This is for you. I can't pass the Weighing of the Heart Ceremony. It was all my fault to begin with!'

'No, Ankhesenamun,' he said to her. 'It was Ay who took my heart, and who separated us from one another. But now, thanks to Charlie, we will live together forever in the Field of Reeds.'

She looked at him, clearly frightened.

'As in life, we will face this test together,' he said, and the pair took a small step forward towards Anubis.

Behind Charlie, the doors to the room swung wide open, and he turned to look at them. On the other side stood his grandmother, beaming proudly. It was time to go.

Charlie looked back towards Tutankhamun and Ankhesenamun, who looked over their shoulders and smiled before turning back to face the gods.

Charlie watched them walk away and then stepped out through the doors to take his grandma's hand.

She hugged him tight. 'I knew you could do it!' she said. 'This is a victory for order over chaos. A victory for The Guardians,' she said. 'And a defeat for...*them*,' she whispered, looking cautiously around her. As she spoke, the sky above them turned suddenly grey and a roll of thunder made its way across the sky.

'It's time for you to rejoin your friends and go home,' she said to Charlie, looking up at the darkening sky.

'Home,' thought Charlie. He wanted nothing more than to go home. But he didn't want to leave his grandma. 'Will you be ok here?' he asked, joining her in looking up at the gathering clouds.

'Of course!' she said. 'I am perfectly fine here.'

'Can't you come too?' Charlie asked.

She laughed and shook her head. 'No,' she said. 'I belong here.'

'I'll miss you,' said Charlie, feeling tears well up in his eyes.

'I'll miss you too,' she said, hugging him again. 'But I am never far away. And this is not goodbye.'

'Grandad misses you,' said Charlie. 'He lives with me and Mom now.'

'I know,' she said, looking pleased. 'You just look after him for me. I'll see him soon enough.'

Charlie felt afraid. He didn't want to lose his grandad.

'It's not his time yet,' his grandma said to him, answering his thoughts. 'There is no need to worry. Everything happens as it's meant to.'

She hugged him again, and Charlie held her tight. 'I'll see you again, Grandma,' he said.

'Indeed you will,' she replied. 'But not too soon!'

Then it felt to Charlie as though he had been pushed, and he was falling endlessly through the air. As he fell, he didn't feel heavy but instead felt light, like a feather drifting in the breeze. And then he landed, suddenly and with a thud, and he was back in the desert, looking up at the tops of the pyramids. They were dark against the blinding sun.

'Charlie!' yelled Sheena gleefully as he coughed and spluttered.

Charlie could see the faces of his three friends looking down at him. He blinked against the brightness of the sun. 'There was a light,' he said, looking up at the pyramid. 'I remember seeing a light.'

'We saw it too,' said George, nodding. 'We don't know what it was, but you seemed to think you needed to reach it.'

'Then we watched the lightning get worse all around you,' added Paige. 'And then...then you fell.'

Charlie thought about everything that had happened. 'The Guardians said I'd be shown the way,' he said. 'But I never thought they were going to kill me.' He coughed again, and tried to get to his feet.

'You made it!' said Paige, helping him to stand. 'You made it!'

For the first time in their whole friendship, George lost his calm. 'Don't you ever do that to me again, Charlie Swain!' he said, the relief evident in his voice. 'We thought you'd died! And you're my friend,' he added quietly.

Charlie moved over to George and put his arm around his shoulder. 'I'm sorry,' he said, feeling sad that he had frightened his closest and dearest friends. 'I did die,' he said. 'But I'm back now.'

George looked down at the sand.

'Is that a tear?' asked Sheena, looking at George.

'No,' said George. 'It is not.' But he turned his back to them all, just for a moment.

'Did you get the incantation to take us home?' asked Sheena.

'I don't know,' replied Charlie, unzipping his bag. 'I hope so.'

He opened the book, holding his breath but he needn't have worried. There, on the page before him was a new map, pointing out the location of the portal they needed. It was one of the archways within the long causeway that ran all the way from the Sphinx to Khafre's pyramid. Next to the map, in beautiful blue letters, was the incantation.

'I did it!' said Charlie, feeling surprised even though he knew everything that had happened.

Nearby, George nodded. 'I knew you would.'

They all fell silent, as they thought about their adventure.

'Let's go,' said Charlie. 'It's time to go home.'

The others followed Charlie quietly to the archway and when they arrived, they all took a moment to look out across the Giza plateau.

'It really is amazing,' sighed George as he gazed at the Great Pyramid.

'Ancient Egypt,' said Sheena.

'And we were here,' added Paige.

They all smiled at one another.

'Are we ready?' asked Charlie.

'Don't we have to wait for sunrise?' asked Sheena.

'Not according to the book,' said Charlie. 'It seems any time is fine to go home.'

'Should we write down the incantation, then?' asked Paige. 'So we can all see it?'

'There's no need,' replied Charlie. 'You'll remember this one.'

'What is it then?' asked George.

Hold hands, said Charlie. And repeat after me. 'Though we know we're free to roam, our quest is done, now take us home.'

They did as they were asked and the little group repeated the incantation three times.

'No one let go,' Charlie reminded them as the archway turned glassy and mirror-like.

'There we are, in the mirror!' said George.

'Let's go!' said Sheena.

'No!' Charlie told them. 'Not yet - wait for them to call us.'

They stood and watched as the four friends on the other side beckoned them through and called them home.

'Now!' said Charlie, and they all stepped through together.

A second later, and Charlie, Paige, Sheena and George found themselves tumbling onto the soft grass that surrounded the abbey archway at the far end of Crankhall Lane. They looked around them and started laughing in relief.

'More than once I thought we were going to have to stay in ancient Egypt forever!' said Paige, lying out on the grass.

'Me too,' said George.

'It was certainly close!' said Sheena.

Charlie thought about everything that had happened, and all he'd been through. 'I wasn't sure we were going to get home either,' admitted Charlie. 'But now we are home, I know I've had the time of my life!'

'Me too,' admitted Paige. 'It's been some adventure!'

'Do you think we'll ever get to go through the portal again?' asked Sheena.

'Who knows?' said Charlie.

'Why don't we look in the book?' suggested George. 'Maybe it'll tell us.'

They gathered around as Charlie excitedly pulled the book from his bag and opened it. Then he looked at them all, a gleam in his eye.

'Well?' asked Paige. 'What does it say?'

Charlie looked at his three best friends and smiled. 'It says 'Never say never'' he said.

HISTORICAL NOTE

Much of the information in this story is true.

Egypt traditionally had many different gods and the Egyptians believed that worship of them all was necessary in order to maintain order and to keep Egypt stable, safe and prosperous. However, Tutankhamun's father, Akhenaten, chose to worship only one god - the Aten (or the sun disc).

He changed his name from Amenhotep IV to Akhenaten, built temples to the Aten, closed down temples to the other gods, and even moved the capital of Egypt from Thebes (modern day Luxor) to modern day Amarna. This new capital city, he called Akhetaten.

Before the reign of Akhenaten, Amun (or Amun-Ra), the sun god, was Egypt's chief god, and there were many temples built in his name and many priests who served him. Through the generations, the priests of Amun had become extremely wealthy and powerful as his temples had gained money, land and influence. When Akhenaten came to power, the priests of Amun lost their wealth and position.

Not surprisingly, many did not appreciate Akhenaten's changes and believed that Egypt would pay for abandoning the gods. In fact, it seems Akhenaten neglected many of his royal duties, and the Egyptian army, used to endless victories, began to suffer defeats.

Akhenaten's closest advisor (his vizier), was Ay. During his reign, he also made Horemheb commander of the Egyptian army. Interestingly, Akhenaten's relationship with Ay seems to have been a close one, and Ay was given permission to build a tomb for himself in Egypt's new capital city.

Akhenaten decorated the new capital with art and statues, and with temples to the Aten. The art of this period was unusual, and Akhenaten is commonly shown with a long head and wide hips. His family are typically shown in the same way.

Akhenaten had more than one wife, including the famous Nefertiti, with whom he had several children, including Meritaten and Ankhesenamun, who became Tutankhamun's wife. It is thought that Tutankhamun's mother was not Nefertiti, but another of Akhenaten's wives, which means Tutankhamun married his half sister. This was common amongst the ruling families of ancient Egypt.

There is some confusion over what happened immediately after the death of Akhenaten but it seems Tutankhamun did not immediately succeed his father. It is not clear whether there were one or two successors to Akhenaten before Tutankhamun became Pharaoh, but what is clear is that Tutankhamun came to the throne at a very young age (he was probably around nine years old). As a result, Tutankhamun was probably very heavily advised by his vizier, Ay, and by Horemheb, the General of the army.

During Tutankhamun's reign, worship of the traditional gods was restored. Temples to Amun were reopened, priests of Amun were put back into their positions of power, the capital of Egypt was returned to Thebes, and Tutankhaten (living image of the Aten) became Tutankhamun (living image of Amun).

Upon his death, somewhere around the age of nineteen, Tutankhamun's widow, Ankhesenamun, does seem to have married Ay. A series of letters written to a neighbouring king appear to show a desperate Ankhesenamun asking him to send her one of his sons as a husband to spare her from having to marry Ay. It seems the king did indeed send his son but he was killed on the way to Egypt, and Ankhesenamun's fate was sealed.

Ay did take the throne after Tutankhamun and was himself succeeded by Horemheb. Horemheb appears to have spent his reign doing all he could to wipe out any reference to his immediate predecessors. It is said he was so good at doing this that many later generations didn't know Akhenaten, Tutankhamun, or Ay, had ruled at all.

The untimely nature of Tutankhamun's death meant that his own tomb was not ready when he died, and he appears to have been buried in a tomb originally intended for someone else. As was customary, Tutankhamun's body was mummified, a death mask was placed upon his head, and he was buried in a sarcophagus (a Greek word, meaning 'flesh eater'), in a tomb with images which showed Ay performing the Opening of the Mouth Ritual for the Pharaoh.

The tomb itself was in the Valley of the Kings and, unlike many other tombs in the same location, it avoided being completely emptied by tomb robbers. Although the tomb was broken into in antiquity, Tutankhamun's mummy and most of the items buried with him remained in the tomb. They lay buried for thousands of years, until they were finally rediscovered in 1922 by the British archaeologist Howard Carter.

Scientific examinations of Tutankhamun's mummy have shown there to be a hole in the back of the Pharaoh's skull. He was also buried without his heart, and a number of his ribs appear to have been removed, whilst others are broken. The Pharaoh also had a fractured femur (thigh bone). DNA evidence has led some to suggest that Tutankhamun had a deformed foot and may have had to walk with a cane. Others have also concluded that the Pharaoh had contracted malaria more than once through his life.

The evidence has led to various suggestions about how Tutankhamun died.

Some think the art of Akhenaten's reign, which showed the Pharaoh and his family with unusually long heads and wide hips, may mean the family suffered from some sort of illness or condition. However, after the death of Akhenaten, art became more traditional again. It is possible that the strange art of Akhenaten's reign was simply a change in style rather than an exact depiction of the royal family's appearance.

Nevertheless, some scientists point out that, as a child of parents who were related, Tutankhamun would probably have had a weakened immune system. Malaria would also have weakened him further. This means Tutankhamun could easily have died from natural causes - either illness or injury - from which he simply could not recover.

Some think that Tutankhamun did suffer an accident, perhaps a fall from a chariot, which could explain the broken bones. This may also explain why the heart was removed, since the body may have been in a poor state when it came to be mummified. The missing ribs may have been removed to make it easier to access the heart and remove it from the body.

When the body was placed in the sarcophagus, it was covered in a thick, black substance. Some of this substance had found its way into the break in the femur (thigh bone), leading the famous Egyptologist Dr Zahi Hawass to conclude there was an open wound above the break when he died. He argued that the Pharaoh may have suffered an accident, which led to the broken bone, which itself then became infected. It is this infection that may have killed Tutankhamun.

To confuse matters, some damage to the mummy may have been caused by tomb robbers, or by Carter and his team when they removed it from the sarcophagus. It is not clear whether the hole in the skull or the broken ribs were present when the Pharaoh died, or whether they represent later damage.

One of the most enduring and dramatic suggestions about the young Pharaoh's death is that he was murdered, possibly by a blow to the back of the head. In this scenario, the most obvious culprit is Ay. Ay had access to the Pharaoh, already held immense power as Vizier, and succeeded Tutankhamun to the throne. In addition, many have pointed to the fear shown by Ankhesenamun in her letters as evidence of foul play. It has also been suggested that Ay had the prince who was sent to marry Ankhesenamun murdered, possibly by Horemheb.

In the end, it is for each person to decide for themselves what they think happened to Tutankhamun. Whatever the answer, how he died remains one of the great unanswered questions of history.

Thank you for choosing to read *In the Shadow of the Sphinx.*

If you enjoyed the story, and if you have the time, would you consider leaving me a review on Amazon?

Don't forget, your free desktop wallpaper is waiting for you!

Get it at akwallis.com/free

Let's connect!

www.akwallis.com
Facebook.com/akwallisauthor
Twitter.com/@akwallis113
Pinterest.com/akwallis0113
(here, you will find the book board for *In the Shadow of the Sphinx)*

ACKNOWLEDGEMENTS

Nothing is achieved alone. I am grateful to a number of special people without whom this book would not have been possible.

Thank you to Carl at Extended Imagery (extendedimagery.com) for the wonderful cover, and to Alison May (alison-may.co.uk) for your invaluable feedback and advice on the first draft of this book.

Mia and Callum, my niece and nephew, thank you for giving of your time to offer your thoughts on the book back at the very beginning. You have helped the story grow, and I am grateful to you both.

Thank you to my lovely sister, Zoe Wallis, to Kath Wallis, and to Lindsay Smith for the hours spent editing and proof reading this book. Thank you also to all three of you for your support and encouragement. It means the world.

A special thank you to Kath Wallis. Mom, you have listened to every idea, offered advice, edited every draft, read every word, and encouraged me every step of the way. As ever, your help and support have been invaluable to me. I don't know where I would be without you. Thank you for everything you do.

And my Jay. For all the things, too many to list, that you have done to make writing this book possible, I am eternally grateful. There aren't the words to tell you how much I appreciate your love and support. Just know that I am ever grateful for all you do, and that I could not have done this without you.

Last, but never least, my thanks go out to you, the reader. It is you that will give life to the story in these pages. For a writer is nothing if her words are not read, a story is nothing if it is not heard. And life is nothing if it is not a collaborative effort.

35658646R00160

Printed in Great Britain
by Amazon